"Give it up, [...]

Travis continued, [...] seat is way too small for you to act as if we barely know each other. Snuggle up and make yourself comfortable. It's going to be a long ride."

She relented and allowed herself to find comfort in the warmth of his body. Being that close to him generated enough heat to instantly do away with her shivers. She hated the undeniable fact she could feel emotions for him after all these years. Living so far away had purged the childhood hurt and had transformed her into a take-charge, hard-as-nails businesswoman who prided herself on being completely in control. Very little fazed her or made her cry anymore. In some circles she was referred to as cold, uncaring and even downright heartless.

Yet here she was on a sleigh, getting all torn up over her close proximity to Travis Granger, so much so that her eyes welled up.

Somehow the words *bah humbug* didn't seem right on her lips anymore.

Dear Reader,

Christmas just happens to be my favorite holiday. Some of my fondest memories center around family, friends, amazing dinners and, of course, presents under the tree. It's when the magic of Christmas heals all wounds and brings together those I cherish most. A year without celebrating Christmas is hard for me to imagine.

That's what prompted me to write about Bella Biondi and Travis Granger, the youngest of the Granger men. What if these two childhood best friends were forced to deal with each other but came from opposite sides of the Christmas fence? Could they possibly ever find common ground, or would they simply dig in and never see the magic that's all around them?

I wanted this book to be both poignant and funny, which brought up memories and emotions I thought I'd lost. Instead, I was able to share my memories with my adult children, which only brought us closer. In the rush of our daily lives, we tend to put off taking the time to tell someone we love our own Christmas story. There's so much more to the holiday than buying someone a present or decorating a tree. It's all those past Christmases that make up who we are and what brings us to this moment.

I hope you enjoy reading this story and that it prompts you to share some of your most cherished Christmas memories.

You can visit me at www.maryleo.com, where you'll find some fun facts about Idaho's Teton Valley and my favorite Christmas cookie recipes. You can also find me on Facebook, where I'll keep you informed of my latest books.

Best,

Mary Leo

CHRISTMAS WITH THE RANCHER

—

MARY LEO

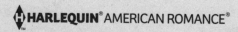

Recycling programs
for this product may
not exist in your area.

ISBN-13: 978-0-373-75549-3

Christmas with the Rancher

Copyright © 2014 by Mary Leo

Printed in U.S.A.

HARLEQUIN®
www.Harlequin.com

ABOUT THE AUTHOR

Mary Leo grew up in south Chicago in the tangle of a big Italian family. She's worked in Hollywood, Las Vegas and in Silicon Valley. Currently she lives in San Diego with her husband, author Terry Watkins, and their sweet kitty, Sophie. Visit her website at maryleo.com.

Books by Mary Leo

HARLEQUIN AMERICAN ROMANCE

FALLING FOR THE COWBOY
AIMING FOR THE COWBOY

This book is dedicated to everyone who rediscovers the magic of Christmas.

Prologue

"This is going to be the best Christmas ever," Bella said as she and Travis leaned out of the small attic window trying to get a better look at downtown Briggs, Idaho.

"That's because I get to spend it with you," Travis whispered.

Bella nudged him, giggling at the absurdity of his statement, as if the magic of Christmas depended on whether or not she was with him.

"That's just silly," she told him.

He shrugged and continued staring out the window leaving Bella to wonder if he really meant it…if his Christmas depended on her.

She hoped not because there was no telling what would happen when they grew up and she'd hate to think that Travis wasn't having a happy Christmas because she wasn't with him.

The thought gave her a shudder.

Or maybe it was the cold seeping in under her shirt.

Twinkling lights decorated every tree and building in the town. Even the giant plaster russet potato perched on the roof of Spud Bank was awash in lights. The life-size heifer in front of Moo Creamery wore a sparkling wreath, and the twenty-foot pine tree in the

town square served as a Christmas anchor for the entire
festive event. It was Bella's favorite time of the year,
and she intended to spend every free minute of it surrounding herself with everything Christmas and that
included Travis Granger, the one boy in the entire town
who loved the magic of Christmas as much as she did.

"It's beautiful from up here," Travis said. "You're
so lucky to live so close to town. You can walk to all
the events. I have to beg my dad or my brother Blake
to drive me in. When I grow up I'm going to move off
that old family ranch and live right here in the city."

Bella slipped away from the window, walked over
to her antique trunk, opened the lid and plopped down
on the floor in front of it. The trunk had once been her
maternal grandmother's hope chest.

"No, you won't. You're a cowboy, and cowboys don't
belong in a crowded city. There's no place to ride a
horse. A cowboy belongs in the country on a ranch."

Travis turned away from the window, closed it and
walked over to her.

"Maybe I don't want to be a cowboy all my life, especially on our ranch where most of the land is dedicated to growing potatoes. Maybe I don't give one lick
about potatoes. Maybe I want to be a carpenter or an
astronaut or even a fireman."

The very idea of Travis Granger wanting to be anything other than what he was born to be gave Bella
a chuckle as she slipped a white lacy jacket over her
long-sleeved red tee, then wrapped a black lace scarf
that had once belonged to her mom's mom around her
neck. She'd never met her grandma, but she loved to
dress up in her old clothes and loved to hear her mom
tell stories of how her gram had married her grandpa

when she was only fifteen because they were in love. Her grandpa was twenty-five.

Her grandma had her first baby while she was still fifteen, but it didn't live more than a few days, her mama had told her. When Bella asked why, she'd told her he was born premature and his little lungs weren't developed yet. Her grandma didn't have another baby until she was almost forty-five. That baby was Bella's mom.

It made Bella feel as though her grandma was still with her whenever she put on her old clothes.

"That's just silly talk. Cowboy blood runs through your veins, just like it does with your dad and your two brothers. There ain't nothin' you can do about changing what's already a fact."

She grabbed her grandpa's black felt cowboy hat that had seen better days and stuck it on Travis's head. According to her dad, her grandpa had worn that hat to church every Sunday for as long as her dad could remember. It didn't quite fit on Travis, falling over his ears, but when he went to pull it off he stopped and thought better of it, knowing darn well how much Bella loved playing dress-up.

He pulled out a piece of white paper from his pocket, unfolded it and showed Bella a sketch of a pretty little ranch-style house.

"Your dad and me have been working on this for a while. What d'ya think?"

"It's pretty, but what is it?"

"It's a house. Don't you know anything?"

She rolled her eyes. "Of course I know it's a house. But whose is it?"

"It's my house, or will be when I build it. Your dad

is teaching me how to make things and as soon as he thinks I'm ready he's going to help me build it. So will my dad and maybe those two cantankerous brothers of mine, if I let them. You can help, too. And you can live there if you want to. It'll be big enough."

"I might consider it if you build an extra room where it's Christmas all year long, even in the summertime."

He snorted and shook his head. "Nobody has a special room just for Christmas. It's not practical."

She stood holding her grandfather's fringed jacket and motioned for him to put it on. It was way too big on him, but Bella still liked the way he looked, like a grown-up rancher going to town. She slipped on the tiara she'd won with her best friend, Jaycee, from when they were eight years old, then glided her feet into a pair of red suede heels her mom had discarded years ago, and pulled a long white skirt that matched her gram's jacket up over her jeans.

Even though Bella was almost thirteen years old and knew other girls her age didn't play dress-up anymore, Bella wasn't ready to give it up. Now more than ever when her parents seemed to be arguing all the time. Sneaking up to the attic and dressing in her grandma's clothes and making up stories about her gram and grandpa was exactly what she liked to do so she didn't have to hear them fight.

"I'll just have to build my own house so I can have a year-round Christmas room," Bella announced.

Travis moved in closer to her. "You don't know the first thing about building a house."

"Then I'll buy one already built with lots of rooms."

He suddenly looked sad. "But I want you to live with me."

"Not if I can't have my Christmas room."

He stepped in even closer. "You can have anything you want. I'll build you two Christmas rooms if that's what it takes."

She leaned in and kissed him right on the lips and immediately felt all warm and sugary. The kiss didn't last more than a few seconds, but she knew they'd be together forever, exactly like her grandma and grandpa.

"Okay, I'll live in your house, Travis Granger, and you can be my boyfriend."

A smile bigger than all of Idaho spread across his soft lips, he took his hat off, placed it over his chest, took her hand and kissed it.

Another sugary tingle zipped up her arm and this time goose bumps danced on her skin.

"I would be delighted, fair maiden."

That's when they heard her mom's stern voice echo up the stairs. "Bella, I need you to come down here right this instant."

Chapter One

Travis Granger stood on the snowy roof of Dream Weaver Inn, holding a string of colored lights in his right hand and a conundrum in his mind. The string of lights were easily dealt with using the hooks he'd installed on the chimney several years ago to accommodate the festive trimming, but the issue of Bella Biondi visiting Briggs after essentially a fifteen-year absence was something this ole cowboy couldn't seem to wrangle his head around.

Despite the fact that he'd briefly seen her a couple of times in the first five years after she'd left with her mom, and never in the last ten, the memory of her had lingered like a habit he couldn't break. None of the women he'd dated—and he'd dated quite a few—tugged on his heart like Bella did. Her dad, Nick Biondi, owner of the inn and close family friend, had kept him up to date with Bella's accomplishments, and the occasional photograph had provided a visual record of how she'd changed from a twelve-year-old tomboy who could ride and rope better than most cowboys, into a twenty-eight-year-old real-estate mogul...a concept that tripped up his memory of her like two bulls living in the same pen.

His fondest recollection was her solid love for everything Christmas. When they were kids, Christmas and the days that led up to it had been elevated to more than just a religious holiday and a visit from the man in a red suit. It meant sleigh rides, ice-skating rinks, caroling in the park, buying or making gifts for just about everyone they knew and magical moments that captured both their imaginations like nothing else. Her family's inn had been the focal point for the entire town during the month of December. Every event seemed to begin and end at Dream Weaver Inn. There had even been a time when Bella had Travis convinced that Santa himself began his long night of deliveries with a stop at the inn for a cup of hot chocolate and a plate of her dad's chunky-fudgy cookies, the absolute best cookies ever.

He didn't know much about her business life out there in Chicago. He'd heard she lived in some fancy condo on north Michigan Avenue, worked 24/7 and rarely took a vacation, probably due to the expense of that high-priced condo. Knowing sweet little Bella, he was dang sure she had to be missing Christmas in Briggs, Idaho. Or why else would she be coming home just days before the main event? He knew her mom had passed away within the last year, and he figured she must be returning to spend the holidays with her dad to soak up some family comfort.

Dream Weaver Inn had hit on some hard times in the past few years with occupancy going down to barely enough to keep the lights on. Travis and his family were trying to change all that, and so far the inn had been coming around with most of the rooms reserved for December and well into January. He was hoping that trend would continue after the holidays, especially now that

Bella might be taking an interest. He wanted to try to keep her around for a while and get to know her again.

As soon as he'd heard about her return he dropped everything else going on in his life to complete the Christmas decorations for her homecoming. He wanted the inn to look exactly as it had before she'd left. It had to be perfect for her arrival that evening, and both he and Nick had worked extra hard to accomplish that goal. If she'd given her dad a few days warning instead of twenty-four hours he probably could have gotten all the repairs to the inn done in time. But as it was, the repairs had to be overlooked in favor of more important things—decorations. He'd even enlisted his dad, his brother Colt, plus his wife, Helen, and their four children, to help in the mad dash to make the inn glow like it had when Bella lived there.

"She's on her way in," Nick hollered up from somewhere below.

Travis couldn't see him as he straddled the roof next to the chimney securing the string of lights around it. Earlier that morning he'd set up the life-size Santa sitting in his sleigh and holding the reins to his reindeer, and once he secured the chimney lights the roof would look exactly as it had when Bella lived there. All he needed were a few more hours and everything would be perfect.

"How close?" Travis called down, as he scratched his chin. He always grew a short beard this time of year, but he never seemed to get used to it. The dang thing itched whenever his nerves got the best of him, and at the moment he wanted nothing more than to shave the thing clean off.

"Said she can see the inn."

Evidently, he didn't have a few more hours.

Travis called back to Nick. "But she's not supposed to arrive until late tonight."

Nick now stood in the front yard out far enough for Travis to see him. He shielded his eyes with his hand as he looked up at Travis. Even though there was a thick layer of clouds hanging over Briggs, the sky, combined with the newly fallen snow, made everything glisten a pearly shade of white. "My girl never was one for clocks. I'm thinking that's her headed our way." He turned slightly and pointed out to the road heading into Briggs.

"Darn it all," Travis cursed. "She always liked to show up early. Be the first one to arrive at a party or an event. I should've remembered that."

His gaze shot across the roof and settled on the road, what he could see of it, and sure enough, a single blue, heavy-duty truck sped its way doing at least seventy-five, with no regard to road conditions or speed limits.

He figured it had to be Bella—she always liked to ride a fast horse. The girl he'd known had been addicted to speed, the acceleration type, not the drug.

A thick blanket of snow had recently covered the valley for as far as Travis could see, turning everything into a white wonderland, exactly the way Travis liked it. The Teton mountain range that spanned the eastern part of the town was shrouded with low-hanging clouds giving the impression they were hills rather than some of the highest peaks in the country. And the normally bustling business section was barely coming to life as a few shopkeepers shoveled the snow off their front sidewalks before their stores opened for business.

"Inn looks good," his brother Colt shouted as he

looked up to the roof from the six-foot high N-O-E-L letters on the massive front lawn. He'd secured them to the ground making sure they wouldn't come tumbling down in the middle of the night, using stakes that Travis had crafted especially for the task. The inn sat at least seventy-five feet back from the street, so any decorations in the front yard had to be larger than life in order for anyone to see them. "Come on down here, little brother, and greet the girl you've been waitin' on for most of your adult life."

Travis hurried to finish up, then he plugged the end of the string into the rest of the lights that surrounded Santa's sleigh. They instantly lit up, assuring him the roof was complete. Now all he had to do was figure out how to get down before she arrived without killing himself, a task that might take some time considering more snow had fallen since he'd first crawled up there. He'd worn a safety harness, and had secured a rope to the ring he'd attached to the roof several years ago, but he sure as heck didn't want to make use of his precaution, especially now when Bella was only minutes away.

He wished he'd have listened to his dad an hour ago when he'd urged him to come on down before the snow got too thick.

But did he listen?

Not this cowboy.

He knew he had to take his time, but adrenaline shot through his veins as the truck quickly approached. Travis could no more slow down his actions than a young boy could stop himself from opening a gift on Christmas morning. Colt was right. Ever since Bella had moved away he'd been anxiously waiting for her permanent return. She was part of Briggs, Idaho, just like he was, and despite her long absence, he knew deep in her heart she could never settle anywhere else. Nothing could get him to admit any of this, at least not to his two older brothers who would have razzed him without mercy.

"She has her own life in Chicago and I have mine right here. I'm excited to see an old friend, is all," he said, knowing darn well his brother knew the truth.

Travis took in a deep breath of the crisp air before he slid his butt down the front side of the roof, his tool belt skidding across the snowy gray shingles as he headed for his ladder at the far end. His hands were about frozen despite his wool gloves and if it wasn't for his new black, genuine beaver cattleman's hat he surely would have frozen into another roof ornament standing next to Santa.

"Whatever you say, little brother, but that *old friend* just pulled up to the front curb. You better get your hustle on or you're going to miss the smile on her pretty little face when she sees the inn all decked out like it used to be."

"I'm moving as fast as I can, considering all the snow that's up here," Travis yelled just as his foot slid out from under him and the only thing that kept him from falling right on his backside was his tight hold on that thick rope.

The sound of small feet running across the wooden porch floor below echoed up to Travis. "Maybe we should've brought that old trampoline, Uncle Travis," Joey, Colt's youngest boy, called up. He'd jumped off the homestead barn roof onto a trampoline on his fourth birthday. Fortunately, Travis had caught him in midair as he'd taken a leap of faith and the two of them had glided down together.

The trampoline might have been a good idea considering Travis couldn't seem to keep his footing on the slick roof.

Unfortunately, he wasn't the kind to admit his shortcomings.

"No need," Travis yelled back. "I've got it all under control." Then he slid another few inches, causing his heart to jump against his chest. His rubber-soled boots took hold on a dry spot on the roof and he let out the breath he'd been holding.

"You best be careful, son," Dodge, his white-haired father, called up to him. "Or you'll be sittin' out Christmas in traction if you fall off that there roof. 'Sides, that girl's been citified. No tellin' how she's gonna react to you, much less her old homestead. Now you get yourself down here in one piece, ya hear?"

"I will," Travis hollered, as he oh-so-carefully tried to maneuver closer to his ladder at the edge of the roof. And darn it all, he was determined to make it down one rung at a time before she walked into the front door of the three-story inn.

DREAM WEAVER INN had loomed out in front of Bella for the last mile, giving her ample time to adjust to seeing it again. Despite the tightness she felt in her chest, the lump in her throat, and the tears she rapidly blinked away, she reminded herself the sight of the inn merely represented another business deal.

Nothing more.

At least that was the mantra she repeated in her head. The inn sat like an anchor at the edge of town with its pitched roof, redbrick chimney, and three stories of Victorian elegance, the absolute perfect inn for Trans-Global Corporation to add to their string of historic inns across the country. She had brokered several inns for TransGlobal during the last year, and it only made sense that her father's inn would be one of them. And if her father hadn't insisted that she show up in person with the paperwork, she could've had the deal sewn up a month ago. Right now she would have been lying on a Florida beach spending some of her commission on fine hotels, expensive wine and gourmet meals, and celebrating her promotion instead of stuck in her old hometown for the next twenty-four hours.

A town she couldn't seem to shake out of her memory.

A town that was holding her back from accepting the promotion at the company she worked for in Chicago.

And most of all, a town where the boy she'd crushed on when she was a kid still held a piece of her heart.

Before she'd left Chicago, she and her shrink had discussed how she would get through seeing the inn, her dad and old friends by concentrating on the task at hand: getting her dad's signature on the bottom line. She'd started seeing a psychologist soon after her mom had died, to help her through the tough times. And recently she'd seen her a few more times to learn some coping skills to deal with seeing her hometown, a place that she still carried a torch for.

Not that she had any intention of acting on those burning feelings.

She knew exactly what she wanted: the corner office at Ewing Inc., which was all but hers. She only needed to complete this million-dollar sale and the CEO position would be hers. Bella was the best man for the job. The board of directors knew it. Her contemporaries knew it. And the retiring CEO knew it. All she had to do now was convince that pesky country heart of hers, a task she'd somewhat accomplished…at least eighty percent of the way. The other twenty percent dripped nostalgia and never wanted to leave Idaho.

She'd come to the conclusion that the less time she spent in Briggs, the better for everyone concerned, especially since it was a week before Christmas, a holiday she'd grown to dislike more than potatoes, and she absolutely loathed potatoes.

Catching an earlier flight into Idaho Falls had been her idea and a good one despite her shrink's caution against it. That way, she could get the papers signed early in the day and drive out of town that evening before her dad had a chance to invite her to a Christmas gala of some kind, which she knew the town would have plenty.

Renting the four-by-four had been another sound decision, considering the weather. If there was one thing Bella understood after living in Chicago for the past fifteen years, it was how to deal with winter. When she'd looked up the predicted weather conditions in Briggs, she knew instantly that anything less would never give her the traction she needed for the frozen roads. Bella prided herself on always being prepared no matter what the situation.

Pulling her rig up to the curb, she immediately spotted her dad standing on the shoveled sidewalk in front of the hideously decorated inn. She couldn't believe he still put up that old Santa and reindeer across the roof. She sighed. It would have to come down and be sold or disposed of before TransGlobal Corporation took ownership. If her father couldn't manage it, well, she'd have to hire someone from town.

A cowboy stood next to giant N-O-E-L letters that she vaguely recognized from her childhood, with a young boy standing next to him, and another older cowboy who looked familiar standing up on the wrap-around porch.

Taking a deep, calming breath and slowly letting it out she turned off the ignition, and slid out of the truck, grabbing her briefcase on the passenger seat. Her bag could stay in the truck. She most certainly wouldn't be spending the night.

"You're a mighty fine sight for these sore eyes," her father said as she quickly walked toward him, careful not to slip on the snow in her new designer boots. She'd hate it if she did something stupid in such an awkward situation.

"Hi, Dad," she said as she reached out and gave him a quick hug. He still looked ruggedly handsome in his fraying jeans, gray parka and black cowboy boots. He still had that familiar scent of musky spices that she'd always loved on him.

She pulled away almost as soon as her face touched his rough cheek, resisting the urge to linger in his embrace. She'd been video-conferencing him from time to time in the past few years, but she'd only seen him in person four times since she and her mom had left Briggs. Each time it had gotten more and more difficult for her to say goodbye.

"Honey, you remember Dodge Granger," her dad told her once they parted. She immediately recognized him and memories of him, his ranch, his barn and his sons all came rushing back.

She quickly pushed them aside.

He went to hug her, but, afraid his bear hug would instantly rekindle their friendship she stuck out her leather-clad hand instead. His big, ungloved hand encircled hers and she instantly felt the warmth of his good nature. She missed men like Dodge, genuinely kind and always willing to help. She was certain hugging the man would melt her resolve, like icicles in sunshine.

"Nice to see you again, Mr. Granger," she told him taking a step back, hoping some distance would help.

"No need to be gettin' so formal, Bella," he said. "Dodge is just fine."

His gruff voice surrounded her memories like a warm blanket. She'd always liked being around Dodge. He'd taught her how to rope before she could ride a horse.

"Dodge it is."

"I'm sure you remember his son Colt," her dad said.

Colt tipped his hat, and held out a hand. He wore a friendly grin that she was sure could charm a girl right into his bed. He looked nothing like the tall, skinny boy she remembered, a boy who needed to grow into his big ears. He had that sexy cowboy look going on that worked on most women her age. Fortunately, not on her. She'd learned to prefer a man in a tailored suit rather than a man in jeans and cowboy boots.

"Hope the drive over wasn't too bad," he said, while standing next to a young boy.

"It was fine, thanks."

He patted the boy's head, mussing up his hair, and the child tried to move away from his touch. Colt grabbed him and the boy squealed with delight.

"This ornery little man is my son Joey."

Joey sucked in his laughter and held out his hand for her. She'd never met a child with real manners. This was a first. She took his small hand in hers. His grip was firm and confidant, better than some executives she'd met.

"Nice to meet you, Ms. Biondi," Joey said while looking into her eyes.

"You, too," she answered, giving him a quick smile.

Small talk had never been her forte.

She had hoped no one but a few guests would be at the inn. Why the Granger men were there stumped her. She had specifically asked her dad to make sure Travis Granger was nowhere near the inn. So why he thought it was okay for the other Grangers to show up was beyond her imagination.

No way did she want to run into Travis.

Ever.

Under no circumstances.

If her dad hadn't agreed to keep him away, she wouldn't have come. No way could she deal with seeing him again…all grown up…wearing butt-hugging jeans and a cowboy hat.

Nope, she could do very nicely without that meeting.

And just as she thought it, there was a loud clatter coming from up above her.

"Look out!" a male voice yelled.

She stared up as a black cowboy hat came tumbling off the roof followed by a man holding on to a thick white rope. He caught himself on the trellis that crept up the front of the building. Then in what seemed like slow motion, he lost his hold and with more hooting he slid off the trellis and reached for a low-hanging branch of the barren maple tree. He only briefly caught it then slid off that and swung toward the front porch. He put out his hands and grabbed hold of the gutter that ran around the roof of the front porch, finally stopping his momentum.

He hung there, strapped in his red harness, momentarily facing the front door.

No one moved or spoke as he slowly swung himself around to face Bella.

"Woo-hoo! That was one hell of an entrance!" he howled.

Despite the stubbly facial hair, something Bella did not usually like on a man, she knew absolutely she was gawking at a grown-up Travis Granger, and from his entrance, grown-up status had obviously completely eluded him.

She lifted an eyebrow, smirked and said, "I'm not impressed."

Although, if truth be told, the little girl in her would have loved to be swinging on the harness with him, but she abruptly quashed that childish notion.

She walked away from him and calmly seized her father's arm, trying her best not to show her anger in front of Travis as she guided her turncoat dad toward the lobby of the inn.

"We need to talk," she told her dad as they padded around the dangling Travis, who smiled over at her looking every bit as sexy as she had imagined he would be. His hair color hadn't changed much from a sandy shade of light brown, only the golden sun streaks were gone and he wore it cropped fairly short now. Despite his having worn a hat, she could tell there was a lot of style going on with all that thick hair.

She'd forgotten how gray his eyes were, the color of

slate, but she hadn't forgotten how his lips had once felt on hers, all warm and sexy. No other boy could kiss like Travis Granger. If he'd improved at all on that thirteen-year-old kiss, which looking at him now he most certainly had to, she definitely needed to get out of Briggs before the ink dried on the documents she wanted her father to sign.

Being around Travis again only deepened the wound in her heart. She'd cried enough tears over him when she first left Briggs. She sure as heck wasn't going to go through that again no matter how perfectly his jeans hugged his butt or how hot he looked dangling in a harness.

TRAVIS LET OUT another loud whoop once Colt and Dodge rescued him. Bella had disappeared into the inn with her dad and Joey, who had followed close behind.

"That woman is a different kind of fine," Travis cooed, every cell in his body excited about seeing Bella again.

Bella Biondi had grown into a siren of an Italian beauty with thick black hair, smokin' hot eyes and an attitude that made him want to know exactly what she kept hidden under all that bluster.

"Maybe so, but that *fine* lady doesn't seem to want any part of you," Colt told him as he helped brush off the snow that Travis was covered in.

"There's where you're wrong, brother. She's begging me to break through that hard shell of hers," Travis said as he retrieved his hat and dusted off the snow.

"I'm thinking that there shell of hers is thicker than twelve-gauge steel, son," Dodge said. "You're gonna need a blowtorch to get through it. And in the end, you might be the one gettin' burned."

"I've never been afraid of a little heat," Travis joked. "It keeps things moving along at a fast pace."

Dodge opened the front door to the inn and the three men walked inside, with Travis honed in on Bella who had removed her coat and knit hat. She looked even more dazzling in a red sweater and tight jeans that showed off every curve of her lean body.

"Everyone, please stop decorating!" Bella announced to Helen, Colt's wife, and their four kids who were busy trimming the monster blue spruce centered in the front bank of windows. Colt's toddler must have gotten scared because she dropped the glass ornament she'd been holding. It shattered on the floor and she began to cry.

Her mom whisked her up and comforted her, but there was no calming the tearful child.

Helen threw Bella an angry look and immediately took the children into the empty back dining room. Most of the guests left for the day right after breakfast, so the inn was always deserted in the afternoons.

"That might have been a little harsh, honey," Nick said, but Bella didn't flinch.

"I'm sorry, but we have a flight out of here this evening. Decorating is a waste of everyone's time. Of course, you already knew that, Dad, so I don't get all of this."

She opened her black briefcase, pulled out a stack of papers, and carefully placed them on a coffee table in front of the tufted brown leather sofa.

"He wanted everything to be perfect for you," Travis

said. "We've been working round the clock to make the inn look like it did when you were a kid."

"Excuse me," Colt said and followed after his wife and children into the back dining room. Dodge retreated out the front door.

"Thanks, but that, too, was a total waste of everyone's time. There will be no Christmas celebrations at the inn this year." She said it as though she had the final word on the issue instead of Nick.

Travis immediately turned to Nick who placed an elbow on the black walnut mantel at the far end of the room. A fire roared in the hearth behind him, warming the festive room. Nick didn't flinch, smile or react. He merely stared at his daughter, stone-faced.

Travis decided to take another approach, rubbed his now itchy chin and spread a friendly smile across his face. "I don't know what you might have planned, but that's not exactly an option. Your dad and half the town have been gearing up for this Christmas for the last six months. The inn is booked to eighty percent capacity, and every event that takes place in this town for the next week all begin and end right here. It's going to be the best Christmas Dream Weaver Inn has ever known."

She folded her arms across her chest, and stuck out a hip. "Apparently my dad hasn't told anyone that he's sold the inn. I've brought the paperwork he needs to sign to make it official, but that's only a formality."

Travis felt as if he'd been sucker-punched in the gut. "That can't be true. There's some misunderstanding. Your dad wouldn't sell his inn and not tell me. I've been repairing it—" That stopped him cold and he turned to face Nick. "You didn't have me put in all that time, all that work so you could sell it, did you? What's she talking about, Nick? You sold the inn? It can't be true. You love this place. The town loves this place."

"It's complicated," Nick said and plopped down on the sofa, running a hand through his graying brown hair.

Travis stood his ground. He had a lot invested in this Christmas and most of the planned events were his doing. He was not about to walk away and let hard-shelled Bella Biondi swipe everything away with her paperwork and city boots, no matter how *fine* she happened to look. He had a sinking feeling even a blowtorch wasn't quite strong enough to get through to her. A flamethrower might be the weapon of choice.

Travis walked right up to Bella, stared into those gorgeous smoky eyes of hers, turned on the charm as thick as molasses and said, "Define complicated."

Chapter Two

"This is none of your business, Travis," Bella said, looking straight into his eyes, as if she could see right through him. As if he was made out of cellophane.

"None of my business? I just spent the better half of two months repairing this place. Not to mention the effort my entire family made to decorate the inn for this holiday, and my sister-in-law Maggie launched a huge ad campaign to drum up business. The place is booked solid for the next two months and you think it's none of my business? I think I have a right to know what's going on and if this 'sale' you two are talking about is true."

"Tell him, Dad," Bella said turning to Nick who sat forward on the sofa as if it were his launching pad and he was about to take off.

"It's true. I agreed to sell the inn." His voice squeaked like an old rusty door hinge. Travis had a sinking feeling even Nick didn't quite believe his own words.

No one spoke while Travis attempted to absorb the full effect of what was now finally sinking in as real.

"Wow. I never saw this train coming. And to think I was excited about your visit." He slid his hat back on his head then moved it forward again, something he seemed to do whenever he found himself staring down a problem of major proportions. This here certainly con- stituted one of those moments.

"Can't imagine why you would be," she added, sounding as if his feelings didn't matter.

The statement lay on him like a wet blanket on a cold morning.

He faced Bella. "A lot has changed since the last time I saw you."

"We grew up."

"Is that what you think this is?"

"Some of us matured, like fine wine."

"Never could see all the fuss. I'm more of a beer man, myself."

She looked him over and he felt a bit naked. "It shows."

"I'll take that as a compliment."

"You're twisting my words."

"You're twisting my heart."

"That would mean you still have one."

"Darlin', the lack of a heart seems to be your afflic- tion, not mine."

"There are no emotions in good business. It's all about the bottom line."

He stared at her pretty face—those smoky eyes, those full lips—and realized she had not only grown up but she had turned into someone he no longer rec- ognized or wanted to know.

"You're right," he said, convinced now there was lit- tle hope of trying to understand the situation. "This is none of my business and I'll be leaving you two to it."

He turned to leave.

"Wait! Travis, don't go," Nick called after him, but Travis no longer wanted to play their game. She'd won this round and he simply had to learn how to cope with the facts. There would be no Christmas at Dream Weaver Inn this year.

Travis headed straight for the front door, opened it and walked outside into the cold, gently closing the door behind him.

NICK STOOD. A look of anger crossed his face. Bella was prepared for anything he wanted to throw at her. She hadn't flown all the way out here to be rolled over by her dad and Travis Granger. This was the biggest and most lucrative deal she'd ever put together. There were eight inns across the country involved in this sale, and TransGlobal intended to add five more in the near future. She had the paperwork for the first seven signed by the owners and ready to go. Her father's signature was all that stood between her and the final sale. It meant everything to her—not only the promotion, but it also affected her credibility in the eyes of high-end clients. Then there was the commission. It was enough to move her into a penthouse on the Golden Mile in Chicago, something she had worked hard to achieve. Something her mom would have been proud of and something her dad obviously did not completely appreciate…yet.

She was sure he'd come around once she had time to show him all this deal would mean both financially and emotionally to both of them.

She'd have to educate him on the finer elements of business, something her dad had never been very good at.

"Now maybe we can get these papers signed."

She deliberately sat down across from him on one of the well-worn leather club chairs, and straightened out the documents he needed to approve, then she pulled out her Princess Grace De Monaco Mont Blanc pen. It was a pricey present to herself for putting this deal together.

The scent of pine from the blue spruce tree mixed with the aroma of the logs burning in the hearth exploded a memory that stopped her cold.

She couldn't have been more than four or five years old. It was Christmas morning and she, her mom and dad had walked into their living quarters up on the third floor to open presents. It was the year she'd gotten her first grown-up doll, one all dressed up in a black business suit, high heels and carrying a briefcase. She remembered how disappointed she'd been when she opened the box and how excited her mom seemed to be about the doll. Bella had wanted a grown-up doll dressed like a cowgirl, with tiny cowgirl boots, a cowgirl hat, carrying a lariat. She'd specifically asked Santa for that doll, and had cried for days over not getting it.

That was the Christmas she'd stopped believing in Santa.

"I'm not going to sign anything I haven't read first."

Her father used his stern, unwavering voice, but it didn't scare Bella. When she was a kid, that voice had always struck a chord of fear inside her and she'd instantly relent to his demands.

But she wasn't a kid anymore.

"Don't be silly. I have your best interest in mind."

"That's your mama talking."

"She was right. You should have sold the inn years ago. It's been nothing but a money drain. Because of this deal, you're getting more than market value. You stand to make a very nice profit."

She placed her pen down in front of him. The tiny

pink topaz stone on the clip caught the light from the fireplace and she thought about what a good purchase that pen had been, that she'd deserved to have something this pretty after all the long hours and hard work she'd put in. At least she'd learned perseverance from him, and for that she would always be grateful.

"That may be true, but it's my offer to read before I sign."

Agitation clawed at Bella's stomach as a clock tick-ticked in the background, a truly annoying sound. "I don't have time for this, Dad. We need to be on our way out of here in less than two hours."

"And who's going to run my inn when I go running off to Orlando?"

"Tampa."

"Whatever."

"You should have closed it weeks ago like I asked you to."

"I couldn't. I have guests booked who are looking forward to their stay."

"That's not your problem."

Her dad shook his head. "It's Christmas, Bella. I can't do that."

"Surely there's someone on your staff who can take charge."

"Wouldn't be fair to my employees. What you're asking me to do is impossible. I can leave for one or two nights, but not like this. Not for good. And not a week before Christmas. They all have their own families to attend to. They can't be doing my job as well as their own."

She rose and began pacing the wooden floor, each step echoing throughout the lobby. She walked over to the baby grand piano in the corner, then back again. There had to be a solution to this dilemma. She refused to stay in this town one more minute than she had to. Already she could feel her resolve waning, especially after her encounter with Travis. His very presence had tugged on her heart.

The front door opened and a young couple walked in, smiling and nodding their greeting as they headed up the stairway at the back of the lobby, the old wooden stairs creaking as they climbed.

Bella waited to reply to her dad until the guests were far enough away. Then she said, "Pay them time and a half for a couple days."

"I won't be solving this by throwing money around. Besides, what's the hurry? I might be able to get someone to take charge in a couple days at their normal pay once that person prepares for it, but not today. And didn't you tell me this would be a smooth transition and my guests would never know the difference? Throwing them out only days before Christmas isn't exactly a 'smooth transition.'"

She'd been having some emotional trouble with that aspect, as well. TransGlobal had decided to gut each inn in order to give them their own unique look. That would require shutting down Dream Weaver Inn during the renovations, something she wasn't exactly ready to spring on her dad just yet. She had envisioned never telling him the details of the sale, figuring once he was settled in his fabulous new condo, enjoying the warm weather and the sandy beaches he'd never think about this silly inn again.

She was counting on it.

"Dad, this wouldn't be a problem if you had cancelled all the reservations and told your guests the truth. TransGlobal is a customer-satisfaction company, meaning the customer always comes first. They pride themselves with five-star service and ambiance." She hoped her logic and calmer disposition would have the effect she needed.

"Well, then, taking their lead, there's no rush to boot everyone out of here and make them uncomfortable." He picked up the paperwork. "I'll just take these here documents up to my room and start reading. We can meet tonight at Belly Up for a steak and I'll hand over the signed docs. But first we should apologize to Travis. He put a lot of work into this place. TransGlobal's getting a nice piece of property."

She wasn't liking any of this, especially the part about kowtowing to Travis Granger. She didn't want to see him again, much less tell him she was sorry for anything.

"If you want to apologize, go right ahead. I still contend this is none of his business. And as far as my staying, that's out of the question."

"You can go on ahead and leave if you want to. But you'll be leaving without me or this deal."

She watched as he walked to the front door, slid his coat off one of the brass hooks and slipped it on completely ignoring her, and trumping her ultimatum.

She let out a frustrated sigh. "Fine! I'll change our flight, but it's only for one more night as long as you can promise me I won't have to see Travis again."

"That boy's been a part of this family since he was a kid and I don't want him feeling as if that's changed none. Whether you see him again or not isn't something I can control. It's a small town."

She pulled in a deep breath and slowly let it out trying with everything that was in her not to simply walk out to her truck, start it up and never look back. She should get someone else to handle her dad. That would be the smart thing to do...the prudent thing...the best thing for everyone concerned.

But she knew she couldn't do that.

"All right! Have it your way. I'll stay overnight. In the meantime, I have no idea if we can get on another flight out of here tomorrow, but I'll try."

"I'm sure you will. And if you can't, we'll fly out the next day or the next. I'm in no hurry."

"I have to meet with TransGlobal on Christmas Eve at my office in Chicago with all the paperwork signed. Nothing can get in the way of that."

He gave her a dismissive hand wave. "Not a problem. We have an entire week. Seven full days." And he walked out the door leaving her to doubt herself for agreeing to spend the night in Briggs...where just about anything could happen.

Travis busied himself with securing a life-size reindeer to the bed of his pickup as Nick approached. He had hoped to get out of there without having to speak to Nick again, fearing he might say something to him he'd regret later. If only that darn reindeer had cooperated and Colt hadn't partially secured it to the front lawn. When Colt did something, he made sure it was done right the first time.

Dang him!

"I've got nothing to say to you, Nick. So you might as well turn right around and head back inside and pack."

"Now hold on there, son. It's not how you think."

Travis stopped pulling on the rope he was using to secure the reindeer and looked across the truck bed at Nick. "No matter what I think, it's none of my business. Bella made that crystal clear."

"You can't take what that girl says to heart."

"All I can go on is what she says, and so far it's been nothing but grief."

"We need to give her time to readjust to Briggs, to me and to you. Right now she's still running on big-city time. It's all she's known for the past fifteen years. It's going to take a few days for all that citified haughtiness to disappear."

"And how does that work if you two are leaving today?"

Nick smirked, and shoved his hands in his jacket pockets. "That's been put off."

Travis picked up his toolbox from the snowy ground and placed it inside the truck bed next to the reindeer's head along with the now coiled rope and harness from the roof. He was ready to leave, but he knew Nick had other plans for him, plans he didn't want anything to do with.

"How'd you manage that? Tie her to the tree or something? She seemed pretty hell bent on leaving."

"Told her I had to read the paperwork before I'd sign anything."

Travis opened the door on the driver's side of his truck. "Great, so that takes a couple hours."

"No, you're not understanding."

"I think I understand everything just fine. You agreed to sell your inn to make your daughter happy even if it means you'll be miserable. I get it. A parent will sacrifice everything for their kids. The thing I don't get is why you didn't tell me before I enlisted my family and half the town to help save your inn when you knew all along you were getting ready to sell it. That's not like you, Nick."

"That's not why you've got your spurs in a knot. You're mad 'cause you had your heart set on spending this Christmas with Bella, like you did when you two were kids. And she can't get out of here fast enough."

Travis always wore his heart on his sleeve when it came to Bella and anyone with half a brain could see it…except maybe Bella. Well, this time he wasn't going to admit to those emotions. This time he wasn't going to be made the fool.

"There's where you're wrong. I couldn't care less if Bella stays or goes. It's the inn I'm upset over."

Travis made himself comfortable behind the wheel of his silver pickup, turned over the ignition, ready to blow this mess. He'd had enough.

Nick came around to his side. "That's just it. I'm trying to save my inn, and show my daughter what she's been missing here in Briggs. I thought a little welcome-home party at Belly Up might help."

"The state she's in, she'd never agree to it."

"No need to tell her every detail."

"And when are you planning on hosting this little shindig?"

"Tonight, around eight. It would mean a lot to me if you could be there to sort of help her transition along."

"What kind of transition are you talking about?"

"The kind where she decides to hang around for a spell, rekindle her love for Briggs and realizes this here inn is part of her heritage and can't be sold…at least not now."

"And how am I supposed to accomplish this miracle when she's so bound and determined to get her way?"

"Show her what she's been missing. Country's part of her soul no matter how citified she might be on the outside. All you have to do is help bubble it up to the surface."

"Like that's even possible."

"I have complete faith in you. Besides, you're my only hope."

Travis saw the desperation in Nick's eyes. The man was like a second dad to Travis and he hated to see him in this pickle with his daughter.

"I'm not saying I'll do it or that I'll show up tonight, but if I do, don't expect miracles. She's not the girl who left Briggs fifteen years ago. That girl's been replaced with someone I don't recognize. And frankly, I don't much like."

"All you have to do is help me delay her a bit. Remind her of all the good things she loved about Briggs. Get her to lighten up a little. Maybe that'll change her mind."

"There ain't nothin' gonna change her mind. She always did have a strong will. Just like her mama."

"But she's got her daddy's heart. I know it. Give her a chance, Travis. She might surprise you."

"She already has," he said and drove away thinking how he had no intention of showing up at any welcome-home party for Bella Biondi, no matter how sexy she looked in her tight jeans or how much he wanted to kiss those full lips of hers or run his hands… He couldn't get that woman out of his head no matter what she did or said. She'd made a mark on his soul and there wasn't anything he could do about it. He simply had to bide his time until she left, and stay as far away from her as possible.

And that included her darn welcome-home party… at Belly Up…at eight.

"Dang it all," Travis said, slapping the steering wheel, knowing perfectly well he could no more stay away from her than a bronc rider could stop himself from riding an ornery, bucking horse.

THE SNOW HADN'T let up for two hours straight and Bella's high-heeled boots were no match for what had accumulated on the ground. She knew better, but hadn't brought any other shoes with her, never thinking she'd have to walk more than a few feet from her rental to the inn.

Now, as she made her way through town, she focused on the delightful fact that she had been successful at changing their flight reservations. Takeoff was scheduled for 4:45 tomorrow afternoon and it couldn't come fast enough for Bella.

The shops were still open, and Christmas music filled the air as people hustled from one store to another. Moo Creamery still had the life-size heifer standing near the front door. The sparkly wreath around its neck seemed bigger than she remembered with a lot more lights. She preferred the smaller one. It seemed a lot less garish. Inside, every seat was taken with adults and kids enjoying sweet creamy treats. She hesitated for a moment, thinking of how luscious Moo's ice cream had tasted, and thought about going inside and buying a cone until reason stopped her. She didn't eat whole-milk products…way too much fat.

She turned away from the window and continued on toward the tavern. If there was any type of retail slow-down going on in other parts of the country, it certainly wasn't apparent in Briggs, Idaho. Everyone in town appeared to be spending money freely.

The four long blocks to Belly Up not only seemed like ten, but she'd nearly fallen on her butt several times. Then there was the inordinate amount of white lights wrapped around every tree, railing and light post. More lights decorated each shop window and doorway, along with wreaths, mechanical Santas, snowmen and reindeer. When she passed the town square, she noted there was a decorated gazebo that hadn't been there while she was growing up, and the Douglas fir in the middle of the square had grown substantially and now not only sparkled with colored lights and a bright star that adorned the very top, but fist-size brightly colored ornaments hung on almost every branch. She wondered how the town had managed to pay for all of this. It seemed like a complete waste of taxpayers' money that could be better spent on something practical like snow removal.

As that reasonable thought zipped through her head, her feet went out from under her and this time she landed hard, right on her butt. She sat there for a moment, trying to catch her breath. Fortunately, there hadn't been anyone around to catch the embarrassing moment.

"You might try the appropriate footwear next time," Travis said as he offered his gloved hand to help her up. He had startled her and her embarrassment only increased now that she stared up at him.

"My boots are fine. I tripped," she said, knowing perfectly well she'd slipped.

When she couldn't get up on her own, he said, "Are you okay?"

He looked genuinely concerned...or was that amusement?

She gazed up at him as he stood under a streetlight looking all sexy hot in his black hat, red scarf and black wool parka. Snow had gathered on his shoulders and on the brim of his cowboy hat as if he'd been out in the elements for quite some time and Bella wondered what he'd been up to. Had he been following her?

"You might have announced yourself, or were you purposely trying to scare me?"

"Merely walking by and saw you take a tumble."

The smirk never left his face as he leaned over and grabbed her arm.

For a second she felt that warm, sugary glow she'd felt when they'd shared their first kiss. How he always made her feel special, beautiful, as if she was the most important person in his life. Then the cold seeped in through her thin pants and that warm glow turned into the reality of her butt freezing as she sat on the ground.

"I'm fine." She jerked her arm out of his grasp. "I can get up on my own, thank you. No broken bones. But why are you following me?"

He stood straight again, looking down at her. That sly smirk still caught on his lips. "That would assume you're worth following, which you are not."

"Then why are you here?"

"To help you up."

"I don't need help."

"Suit yourself," he said with a chuckle and strolled away, leaving her there to deal with the elements and her slippery boots.

"Of all the arrogant, ill-mannered…"

She sighed loud enough for him to hear her, but he didn't turn around.

TEN MINUTES LATER, with her pride still stinging, Bella pulled open the heavy glass door to Belly Up Tavern. The one and only time she'd been inside, it was with her mom on the morning they'd driven out of town for good. It was Christmas Eve morning and Bella had had no idea they weren't coming back.

Her mom had stopped in to pick up her final paycheck. Not only had she kept the books for their inn, but she'd also doubled as a bookkeeper for a few of the businesses in town. That extra work had served her well, considering she landed a CFO position at a top company in Chicago a mere six years later.

Dream Weaver Inn had been her dad's dream, not her mom's, and the inn always operated at a loss. Still did, thus the reason it was time to sell the place. Walking into the tavern now, with Christmas decorations hanging from every beam and light fixture only brought the memory full circle. She was finally going to be rid of that darn inn and all the memories that went along with it once and for all.

She longed to get this thing over with. She'd placate her dad by agreeing to share a meal with him for old times' sake, maybe share a bottle of red wine, collect the signed offer and they'd be out of town in less than twenty-four hours. If her dad didn't want to join her then so be it. He could fly out later, alone. She intended to be on that flight out of Idaho tomorrow afternoon, and there was absolutely nothing that would stop her.

"Surprise!"

At least fifty complete strangers stared at her seemingly waiting for her reply. At once she turned back to the door to check out who had stepped inside after her, but there was no one. The "surprise" had been for her. She stood staring at all the smiling, happy faces feeling like a deer caught in the headlights, too stunned to physically move.

Who are these people?

Then, slowly, as if the picture in front of her began to focus, she could pick out familiar faces and realized the strangers were some of her closest friends from childhood.

"Oh, my God! You guys," she said completely dumbfounded by their exuberance.

She was going to kill her father, who was noticeably absent from the lively group. Probably a smart move on his part considering the anger she felt towards him knowing the "steak dinner" was simply a rouse.

And she fell for it....

At once the group bombarded her with questions and old jokes. She had a hard time keeping up as she tried to be polite. Unfortunately, she didn't recognize anyone right off or remember their names. She had little desire to rekindle friendships or to get the dirt on any of her fellow classmates which seemed to be what most of the group wanted to share, along with their business cards and contact information.

She graciously took their cards, wrote down other pertinent info, and shared her own contact information knowing perfectly well from her past experience with these fair-weather friends that none of them would follow through. Once she drove out of town that would be the end of it, exactly how it had been when she and her mom drove out of town fifteen years ago.

For the next several hours Bella bounced from one parochial conversation to the next with people she'd all but forgotten. Even her childhood best friend, Jaycee Barnes, now mother to two boys and a girl, initially only stirred up a mild amount of nostalgia. Then, as if a switch had turned on inside Bella, the more they shared their lives the more she genuinely missed their friendship. She'd never bonded with another girlfriend like she had with Jaycee. They had been more than best friends; they had been sisters.

Jaycee looked tired. Gone was her waist-length chestnut-brown hair, replaced by a short cut that had lost all its bounce. She wore a plain blue Western-style shirt, black jeans and well-worn tan-colored cowgirl boots. She carried an alert baby girl on one hip, dressed in a red Santa outfit with a white stretchy headband around her little head that sported a spray of mini round ornaments that bounced every time the baby moved.

"You brought your baby to a bar?" Bella asked once the two women had settled on bar stools. They sat at the end of the long wooden bar, farthest away from the front door and the Christmas tree that dominated the picture window adjacent to it. Bella was working on her third longneck beer while Jaycee sipped a club soda with several limes. They had chatted about her children for a good ten minutes and now Bella wanted to move onto another subject. Children were fine, as long as Bella didn't have to interact with them or listen to gloating parents... Jaycee was beyond gloating and well into exulting.

For one thing, Bella had a hard time believing anyone

would want to bring their "cherished" baby to a bar let alone want to nurse said baby while sitting on a bar stool.

"It's family owned," Jaycee said, as she cradled her baby under a small pink coverlet with a strap that she'd slipped over her head that kept both baby and nursing mama hidden.

It wasn't as if Jaycee had whipped out a breast to feed her baby or anything equally uncomfortable for everyone else…but still.

A bar!

"And that means…?"

"It's not like it's a regular bar-bar where singles troll for a pick up."

"Didn't you just tell me you met your husband in this bar?"

"That was different. Fred wasn't trolling. He was here on business."

"What kind of business could have brought him to Briggs?"

"Fred works for the National Potato Council."

Bella nodded, and smirked. "Of course he does."

She took a couple swigs of her beer while Jaycee droned on.

"It's a good job, but raising three kids is costly. We've been trying to buy a bigger house 'cause we've outgrown the one we're in, especially with another baby coming. I found the perfect one in town, but Fred's been travel-ing so much it's hard to pin him down long enough to get all the paperwork together to put in a proper offer."

Bella nearly choked on her beer. "You're having an-other baby?"

"Yes, isn't it wonderful?" Her girl's hand poked out from under the pink blanket and grabbed her mom's chin.

"Wonderful," Bella lied.

It was one thing to have three kids and be financially strapped, but to be happy about being pregnant with a fourth was simply irrational…at least in Bella's way of thinking.

"Bella, baby, Mommy's trying to have a conversation."

Bella was about to take another pull on her beer when she focused on Jaycee's words. "You named your baby Bella?"

Jaycee nodded, and a wide grin spread across her haggard-looking face. "You're my best friend. Isn't that what best friends do? I'm sure when you have your own baby girl you'll name her Jaycee. You don't have to if you really don't want to. I won't be offended, I promise, but that's the promise we made to each other when we won the tiaras."

Bella suddenly remembered they'd tied for Miss Junior Russet when they were eight years old, the same day they'd promised each other to name their first baby girl after each other. It was the first time in the history of the pageant that there'd been a tie and Jaycee thought they should do something special to commemorate the occasion. Bella had agreed and had treasured that tiara, always keeping it prominently displayed in her room.

But when it came time for her to leave with her mom, she could only bring two suitcases filled with her things and the tiara didn't make the cut. At the time, she figured she'd be back for her things later, probably in a week or so. Had she known they wouldn't be returning to Briggs anytime soon, she would've brought her tiara with her. It had been one of her favorite things. She had no idea what happened to it and hadn't thought about it in years.

"That was a long time ago. We haven't spoken to each other since we were kids. How can we possibly still be best friends?"

Jaycee threw Bella a look as if she didn't understand the question. "Did you get another best friend?"

Not even close.

"No, but friends keep in touch."

"I figured you were busy, is all. I forgave you for not answering my letters."

"You forgave me? You sent me one letter telling me how Travis had started hanging around with the popular girls in school and when I asked you to be more specific you never wrote back."

The news that Travis had moved on so quickly had devastated Bella and had taken her a long time to get over the hurt.

Jaycee took a sip of her drink. "I wrote back, but you'd already moved. The letter came back to me, unopened with no forwarding address. Besides, I was mad at you for leaving and not telling me first. I eventually forgave you and sent you another letter, but that one came back, as well. Now that I have kids of my own I know exactly how much they misinterpret situations they don't understand. It was your mama's decision to leave, not yours. I just couldn't understand that when I was twelve."

It was true. Bella knew that a twelve-year-old looked at friends and boys much differently than an adult did. And it was also true that she and her mom had moved a lot in the beginning, so she needed to cut Jaycee some slack for the absent letters. And just as a loving warm feeling washed over Bella and she leaned in to tell Jaycee how much she wanted to rekindle thier friendship, a male voice interrupted her.

"As I live and breathe. Little Bella Biondi. Now that's a Christmas miracle."

Bella turned to face a grown up Dusty Spenser, the one boy who could have given Travis a run for his money when they were kids. Dusty had grown into his big hands and feet. He had to be at least six-four with a shock of jet-black hair, the same chiseled nose and baby-blue eyes that used to make her swoon whenever she gazed into them.

Dusty marched right up to her, scooped her up in his strong arms and twirled her around like a cloth doll. As she twirled she spotted Travis, looking as gorgeous as ever in a dark green sweater and tight jeans. She thought she never wanted to see him again since he'd so rudely left her on the ground outside.

Until now.

Now she wanted to be in his arms and not Dusty's, just as she had wanted to be his girlfriend when they were kids, but she knew darn well where that would lead as adults.

Nowhere.

Dusty finally stopped twirling her and plopped her down. Travis stood nearby the buffet table, which featured every combination of potatoes known to mankind. He was staring right at her as he looked up from a conversation he was having with several women Bella recognized as the more popular girls from school. What they were doing at her party, she didn't know. She never liked them, and they never liked her.

Apparently, Travis had a much different relationship. One of the women seemed to be tugging on his hand, while another pulled on his arm to go in the opposite direction. Bella couldn't be sure if he was seriously trying to get away from them or simply flirting. Regardless, she wished he hadn't come to her party.

Granted, seeing her childhood friends had been enjoyable, especially Jaycee who she would like to see again sometime, but that was as far as it went. This town was not her home and these people were no longer her people. She truly didn't fit in anymore. If her dad thought seeing everyone would change her mind about the sale, it had accomplished the exact opposite.

For one thing, Travis seemed to have grown into the man that Jaycee had only mildly described in her letter. Now he seemed to be more of the town stud instead of the school flirt that Jaycee had noted.

Dusty yammered on about how glad he was to see her. How he was a Realtor now, with his own business out of Jackson, Wyoming. He even gave her a card, but all Bella wanted was to get the heck out of there, and not just the tavern, but the entire state.

And as soon as the world stopped spinning, she would do just that.

Chapter Three

"It's the only way you're going to get home without falling on your butt again. Them city boots of yours might look good, but they're worthless in all this snow. Come on." Travis held out his hand. "You don't have to even talk to me if you don't want to."

It had taken Bella the better part of thirty minutes for her world to completely stop spinning after Dusty had given her that twirl. Three beers—or was it four or even five, she'd lost track—combined with no food had given her a buzz she wasn't prepared for. And by the time she was ready to fight the elements, the snow had accumulated to an impossible level. Her only course back to the inn was to either walk, which seemed totally problematic, especially since she'd already fallen once, or she could ride up front with Travis in his red horse-drawn sleigh all lit up like a Christmas tree. Clearly he was taking the season to a whole new level.

The sleigh held not only Travis, which was bad enough, but Dusty, his pretty little wife, Dora, who couldn't be more than five foot two inches tall in heels, bartender Milo Gump, a mountain of a man under a brown cattleman's pinch-front hat, his pink-haired, pregnant wife, Amanda, and Jaycee, without her baby.

Her husband, Fred, had stopped by to take little Bella home right after Jaycee had nursed her, thank you very much. They were all seated inside the covered sleigh, sharing thick wool blankets, looking warm and cozy despite the bitter cold, singing Christmas carols.

Of all the things Bella did not want to do, sitting up front with Travis and sharing a blanket while those two magnificent, perfectly marked, bay-colored Clydesdales with their classic white socks and well-defined blaze faces pulled everyone home, was on the top of her list.

"I can walk. I'll be fine," she told him in no uncertain terms and turned away from the sleigh, facing what had to be the snow challenge of her life.

But Dusty had other ideas.

Before Bella could take one step, he jumped down from the sleigh, picked her up by her waist and deposited her on the red leather coachman's seat next to Travis.

"This is for your own good, darlin'," Dusty said, and a moment later the sleigh was gliding over the snow-laden street heading in the opposite direction from the inn with Bella trying to stay as far away from Travis as possible.

"Come on and move in closer. I won't bite," Travis said while a raucous version of "Sleigh Ride" echoed from the group sitting inside the sleigh.

"No...thanks," she told him, her jaw quivering.

He glanced over at her. "Your stubbornness is going to give you frostbite. You look like you're shaking."

She turned to face him. "You had this planned, didn't you?"

"Sure did."

She crossed her arms over her chest. "I thought so."

"Don't be so dang smug. This has nothing to do with you. I always take them home when I bring my sleigh to town. Just makes sense, especially in all this snow. Nothing personal. Now, slide on over here and get under this blanket before I have to take you to the E.R. for hypothermia."

He moved the reins to one hand and with the other held the blanket up for her to slide under. A fiercely cold breeze slapped her face with snow and her hesitation at once dissipated. She slid over as close as possible without touching him, tucked the blanket over her legs and at once felt warmer.

"Now, isn't that better?"

"It'll do."

The sleigh hit a small drift and suddenly her hips and legs rested against his, the warmth of his body permeating hers.

"Mmm, I like that," he said. "Reminds me of when we used to sit together up in the attic at your place."

"Yeah, well, it's only because we hit a bump in the road."

"I'd say we've hit more than a bump."

She threw him a look, but didn't respond. Her thoughts weren't quite clear at the moment, and she didn't want to say anything that she'd regret later. Instead, she slid away from him until he hit yet another drift and she slid into him once again.

"Give it up, Bella. You're too cold and this seat is way too small for you to act as if we barely know each other. Snuggle up and make yourself comfortable. It's going to be a long ride."

She relented and allowed herself to find comfort in

the warmth of his body, and in so doing she caught herself silently singing a rousing rendition of "Jingle Bells."

Being that close to him generated enough heat to instantly do away with her shivers. She hated the undeniable fact she still had feelings for him despite all the hours she'd cried herself to sleep when she was a teen. Living so far away had purged the childhood hurt, and had transformed her into a take-charge, hard-as-nails businesswoman who prided herself on being completely in control of her emotions. Very little fazed her or made her cry anymore. In some business circles she was even referred to as cold, uncaring and even downright heartless.

Yet here she was getting all torn up over her close proximity to Travis Granger, so much so that her eyes welled up.

And she'd been certain she'd gotten over him years ago.

Yeah, right.

THE NEXT MORNING, Travis awakened early, unable to sleep. All he could think of was Bella Biondi's body rubbing up against his under that blanket in the sleigh. And that smile...*get outta town.* Way too much emotion had been surging through his veins for a sound sleep, especially since he'd spent the night at the inn, only steps away from Bella's room. He'd boarded his horses and stowed his sleigh in the stable behind the inn. It was easier for him to stay in town during the week before Christmas, where Nick always provided a free room.

He'd gotten offers to go home with two childhood classmates who he'd once hung around with after Bella and her mom had left town, but he wasn't interested in lighting a fire under those relationships. Truth be told, he'd never been interested in either one of those women other than as friends, but to this day, they never seemed to get the message.

Until last night when he told each of them flat out, and even then there was the whole "benefits" conversation. A waste of time, he told them.

With Bella back in town, his entire focus had shifted, especially since he'd caught something in her eyes last night while they were riding inside the sleigh: a genuine, unfiltered happiness. More than once he'd spotted her pretty lips mouthing the words to a Christmas carol, as if she had no control over the surge of joy that overtook her. It was that surge he wanted to appeal to. That playfulness he thought he might tap into and keep her right there in Briggs, at least until he could get her to let her guard down and enjoy the holiday he now knew she secretly still loved. No one who truly disliked Christmas would sing along with the group, no matter how cool she acted or what she said.

Sometime around dawn, he'd gotten up, showered, dressed and took off for the only place in this entire town where he might find something that would help bring out that playfulness: the attic inside Dream Weaver Inn. He thought if he could locate the tiara he'd overheard her talking about with Jaycee that maybe he'd be able to help her find Christmas in her heart. He knew she hadn't taken it because he'd wandered into her bedroom right after she'd left and found it lying on the floor next to her bed. At the time, even though Nick had told him she and her mom had moved away, he hadn't believed it. Instead, he assumed they'd be returning one day soon, so he'd picked it up and placed it on her pillow.

Regrettably, she had never returned and her bedroom had later been converted into a guest room. Knowing Nick never threw anything away, Travis hoped the tiara would be somewhere up in the attic and he intended to find it.

A LOUD THUMP awoke Bella much later than she had planned. She'd set the alarm on her phone to go off at precisely seven-fifteen, but unfortunately she'd left her phone in her purse and hadn't heard it go off. The antique metal clock on the nightstand told her it was now almost twelve-thirty in the afternoon. Luckily, she and her dad still had enough time to catch the flight she'd booked if they hustled.

She rolled onto her back and sighed. So far nothing had gone as planned. She reflected on the red sleigh Travis had brought her home in last night.

Did she dream it?

What single guy owned a horse-drawn sleigh?

There was something not quite right about that, and definitely not something she wanted any part of, even though she had to admit Travis had made the experience more fun than she'd expected it to be. Once she'd warmed up and relaxed, she could have ridden next to Travis all night long...of course, she could never admit that to anyone. Especially not to her dad who would rip up the paperwork and sabotage the entire deal.

Besides, that feeling she had last night was merely a moment in time. Not something she could base her future on. She was a city girl now who would soon be achieving her professional dreams. The country part of her had long since been replaced with high-rise buildings, trendy wine bars and corporate meetings. She wanted nothing to do with anyone or anything country and that included Travis Granger and this darn inn.

Another thump and this time she knew it was coming from the attic. She guessed her dad must be up there packing. Not that he had time to pack anything other than his clothes at this point.

Thump. Thump. Thump.

She felt the noise down to her toes and wondered what the other guests were thinking. It had to stop if only for her own selfish reasons.

Bella slipped out of her cozy four-poster bed and peeked out the windows expecting to see that most of the snow had been plowed off the roads, but instead nothing was moving. The roads were still thick with snow and not a car or plow in sight.

This was a catastrophe. She'd never get out of this darn town.

She checked her phone for messages. She had six text messages from her assistant, several emails marked urgent and, along with voice mail from a few of her friends who were undoubtedly inviting her out for a drink, there was one voice mail from her dad.

She rarely listened to voice mail and instead simply returned the call. But since her dad seemed to be up in the attic, calling him was a waste of time.

Instead, she washed up, answered her other messages, combed her hair, patted on some thick concealer to soften the dark circles under her eyes and smeared on a bit of lip gloss to make herself look somewhat decent in the tiny well-appointed bathroom.

She had always loved this room when she was a kid.

It was now the biggest guest room at the inn, but it had served as their living room when she was growing up. It had always been decorated in bright shades of green and gold and it still held that same tradition. The wood was mostly walnut, along with the dark wood floor. Still, because the drapes were a lighter floral and the high ceiling had been purposely kept white, the room gave off a cozy Victorian ambiance. Add to that the gas fireplace which she'd kept going all night long, and the room was positively heaven.

Too bad every stitch of furniture in it would have to be sold. TransGlobal had their own style for their guest rooms and it certainly didn't include antiques. They prided themselves on uniformity and consistency in both service and comfort. Their furniture was identical in every room, along with the bedding, carpeting, drapes and anything else that went into a TransGlobal Inn.

Thump. Thump. Thump.

She slid on the provided white terry robe and slippers and stomped out into the hallway in the direction of the private stairway that led to the attic, ready to confront her dad for his persistent noise.

"Dad! Dad! You're making too much noise." She tried to keep her voice down as she stood at the bottom of the wooden stairs, gazing up at the open doorway to the attic.

"Then maybe you should come on up here and help me move some of this stuff," Travis said as he walked into view.

The man seemed to be everywhere. Was he stalking her?

"What are you doing up there?"

"Looking for this," he said and held out the tiara he'd been holding behind his back.

Without hesitation, Bella took the stairs two at a time. When she arrived at the top Travis handed her the treasure.

"Where did you find it?"

Bella carefully cradled the delicate tiara in her hands.

"Hanging on a nail behind some old pictures. I overheard you talking to Jaycee last night and thought you might like to have it again. It was pretty dusty, but it cleaned up easy."

"It looks beautiful. Thanks."

The rhinestones sparkled against its silver frame. It looked exactly as it had when she first won it, maybe better.

"Your trunk is up here, as well. That's what was making all the noise. Your dad must've moved it up on the rafters and when I brought it down it kind of got away from me."

Bella had all but forgotten about her trunk. Her childhood memories would be tucked inside, even some of her journals. Her stomach tightened just thinking about what she might find in there.

He walked over to the trunk and opened the lid. She hadn't had time to lock it before she left Briggs with her mom. At once she saw her grandmother's white lace suit and a rush of memories flooded her thoughts.

The trunk now sat open in front of the only window in the attic. The window she used to hang out of to see the entire town and the window she and Travis climbed out of at night during the summer so they could stare up at the stars from the roof and talk about their dreams. She had thought those nights would never end.

Silly girl.

Not that she was complaining. Her life in Chicago was great, but she really didn't need constant reminders of all that she'd left behind. What good did it do, anyway? She could never live in Briggs even if she wanted to. Her future was in Chicago where she could flourish. Briggs would only stifle her ambitions.

Besides, there was only one person she cared about in Briggs and that was her dad. No one else mattered. Especially not a bearded Travis Granger who apparently thought so little of himself he didn't even shave in the morning. Why on earth he persisted in that silly beard was beyond her, but it went along with the entire town. No one really cared about fashion or trend.

She wondered why she sometimes still pined over this place.

A total waste of time.

Anger replaced the tightness in her stomach, anger at her parents, but mostly at Travis for finding the stupid tiara and stirring up forgotten memories.

"You should've left it up in the rafters. It's all junk that can be thrown out."

"Don't you want to look at what's inside first?"

"Not particularly." She tossed the tiara inside the trunk, then wandered away without looking at anything else. If she'd lived without the trunk and its contents for all these years, she certainly didn't want anything now. "I need to talk to my dad. I presume he's in the lobby?"

"He told me he called you and left a message on your phone. His staff will cover for him today."

She flashed on her phone messages. "I haven't listened to it yet."

"Well, then, you don't know he drove over to Jackson yesterday before the roads closed. He won't be able to get back until they open again."

The back of her neck ached.

"Any idea when that might happen?"

He shrugged. "Maybe sometime later today, if it doesn't snow again."

The thought of spending yet another night in Briggs caused her stomach to reel, especially if she had to spend it around Travis.

"I need to get home."

"You are home."

"I live hundreds of miles away or didn't you notice?"

"I know where you live, but Briggs will always be your home."

"I was scheduled to leave this so-called 'home' today. I'm not prepared to hang around for any length of time. This isn't how I planned it."

She crossed her arms over her chest hoping the tension she was feeling would dissipate.

It didn't.

He shrugged and grinned, flashing that sexy smile of his, but she was in no mood to be wooed by his charms. "As the saying goes, life is what happens…"

"That might be true, but I don't have time for this."

"Look," he continued. "You might be stuck here for a couple more days. Why not relax and enjoy it? There's a wagon-load of fun events planned. You might actually get a kick out of some of them."

She took a step closer to him, staring right into those sexy gray eyes of his. He smelled clean, masculine. She swallowed and took a deep breath, concentrating on what she wanted to say.

"Let me straighten you out," she told him. "I am not

here to have fun. I'm here to work and put this sale behind me. Nothing and no one is going to stop that from happening."

He stepped in even closer so they were only inches away from each other. "Do you even know how sexy you look when you're giving out ultimatums?"

She refused to give in to his flattery. "Does this work on other women?"

"Never had the need to use that line before."

"A word of advice—it doesn't work. I'm not the least bit intrigued. Matter of fact, I find you annoying."

"That's a good start."

She could feel his breath on her face, soft and warm.

"Believe me, there is no beginning. Just the end."

"Was it a good story?"

"What story?"

"Ours."

She couldn't help the smirk that snuck up on her. "We have no story."

"This is our story. These moments. This encounter. Last night when you clung to me for the entire ride home."

"I had no choice."

"There was plenty of room inside the sleigh. You were free to go on back there whenever you wanted to, but you didn't."

It had never occurred to Bella to move to the back. What could she have been thinking?

That was the problem; she hadn't been. Between the beer, the cold and seeing all her old friends she had operated in some sort of fog.

She could feel her resolve disappearing. She needed to get away from him.

Taking a couple steps back she said, "I didn't like all the singing. But that's beside the point. If I'm stuck here for a few days, I'll need to buy some clothes."

"We can walk to town. I'm sure the shops are open."

"I can do it on my own, thanks."

"I need to go to town, anyway, and besides, you might fall again in those city boots and need someone to give you a lift up."

Her gut told her to insist she go alone, but her mind had other ideas. "I can be ready in twenty minutes."

"Meet you in the lobby."

TRAVIS AND BELLA stepped out the front door of Dream Weaver Inn. Bright sunshine caused everything to glow stinging Travis's eyes as he walked alongside Bella. The air felt crisp and clean. Travis had an inclination to take her hand as they navigated the sidewalk, but then decided he didn't want to push his luck.

He had a hard time believing he and Bella were heading to town together. It had been as easy as pulling a candy cane off a Christmas tree; they hadn't even argued over the matter. It was so easy it got him to wondering if she didn't have something devious stuck up her sleeve.

The first snowball hit Travis in the shoulder. The second snowball hit Bella squarely on top of her head.

"What the heck!" Bella said as she and Travis ducked behind a car parked alongside the curb.

At once Travis could hear the squeal of children laughing and the high-pitched giggle of his niece Scout. No other child had a giggle like Scout.

"You know this means war!" Travis yelled back at the group of children lobbing snowballs at them from across the deserted street.

"Do random children usually pelt people with snow-balls?" Bella asked as she brushed the excess snow from her coat and hair.

Travis compressed a snowball between his gloved hands then lobbed it at the group of kids ducking behind a tall snow bank on the curb.

"These aren't random kids, they're my niece and nephews."

"You're dead meat, Uncle Travis," Buddy, his brother Colt's oldest, yelled. Buddy had recently turned thirteen years old and usually acted as the leader of the group.

"My sisters-in-law must be in town shopping."

"Shouldn't these kids be in school?"

He threw her a look. "Even Chicago must have snow days."

"Of course they do, but…" And just as she said it, three snowballs hit her in succession. "Those little… Alright. Now you guys are in for it," she yelled over to them and started making her own snowballs and lobbing them over at the kids. Of course, none of her snow-balls were very dense, and neither were Travis's. They didn't want to hurt anybody. The fun of it was in the battle, not the score.

Soon there were so many snowballs bouncing back and forth that they were covered in snow and couldn't lob any of their own, so they did the only thing they could.

They ran.

Travis grabbed her hand and they sprinted away as fast as they could, laughing as they headed down the sidewalk toward the shops. When they were far enough away, Bella pleaded with him to stop so she could catch her breath.

"I…need…to…rest," she said taking in great big gulps of air as she bent over and supported her upper body by holding on to her thighs.

"And here I thought you were in shape," Travis said.

She squinted up at him. "Whatever gave you that idea?"

He didn't answer, but merely looked her over with a grin on his face.

"I work out…with weights. I'm not the jogger…type."

"How are you at ice-skating? If I remember correctly, you used to be able to do circles around me."

She finally caught her breath and stood. "What do you have in mind?"

"Skaits Ice Skating Rink is around the corner. Want to give it a whirl?"

"Old man Skaits never took very good care of the ice."

"His sons run the business now. Wait 'til you see it. Come on." He strolled toward the rink hoping she'd follow. The fact that she'd laughed over the snowball fight showed promise, as if the wall she kept around her had formed a crack. He was hoping to bring that wall completely down by the end of the day, or at the very least knock a few bricks off.

"I haven't been on skates since I was a kid. Travis, wait up! I can't do this. Travis!"

But he kept walking and she kept following and before he could hum a few bars of "White Christmas," they were laced up in their rented skates and stepping onto the pristine ice.

As soon as she had both feet on the ice she grabbed his arm for support, a perk he hadn't thought of when he came up with the idea of skating. He loved being this close to her, loved being able to smell her perfume, the scent of her hair, the feel of her body against his. He knew winning her affection would be like trying to catch a raindrop, but dang it all, he couldn't help himself. She'd captured his heart a long time ago, and there was almost nothing she could do or say to free it from her grasp.

"This is crazy," Bella said as she struggled to remain upright.

"It's like riding a horse. Once you learn you never forget."

"Easy for you to say." Her feet went right out from under her and if it wasn't for Travis holding on to her she'd have hit the ice. "I can't do this."

"Sure you can. Loosen up. I can feel how tense you are."

"There are things that just don't come back to you and this is one of them. I want to leave."

They were almost to the center of the ice. Everyone else was skating around the edges with a few brave kids spinning in the center showing off classic moves. Johnny Mathis crooned "Sleigh Ride" over the speakers, and the air buzzed with the chatter and laughter of everyone having fun.

He let go of her and she stood stock-still, afraid to move. "I can't believe you're going to give up that easily. Where's the fight? Where's the drive? If you can't muster up any grit, you'll have to leave on your own, 'cause I'm staying."

"You're not serious."

He skated away. "As serious as a bobcat up a tree."

He joined the group circling the arena and when he came around and saw her again, she was skating in her own circle in the center. Granted, she was moving at a snail's speed, but she was skating.

If Travis knew anything about Bella, he knew nobody was going to tell her that she'd lost her fight. No matter how scared she was of the situation, she would always come back punching. She'd never been the type of person to give up, and ice skating certainly wouldn't be her downfall. When she was a kid she could outskate Travis, his brothers and most of the town.

And just like that, while Travis watched her screw up her courage, she dug in her toe picks and took off on the ice.

He'd known she would eventually let go of all her fears, allowing them to fly away like dandelions in the wind. Within minutes she'd discovered her ice legs and joined the rest of the group as they circled around the rink.

Soon Travis caught up to her. "I never doubted you."

"Then I've taught you well," she said and took off to the center to practice a few simple figure eights along with a couple spins thrown in to prove she still had it in her. At one point she took the time to teach a young girl how to do a few tricks on the ice, and then helped an older woman who couldn't seem to get her footing on the ice. Travis marveled at how she unselfishly helped anyone around her who needed it, a total one-eighty from the girl who wanted to close her dad's inn right before Christmas.

They skated for about two hours, joining forces from time to time, holding hands like they used to when they were kids. Back then Bella liked to show off so they'd do a lot of couples skating, but now holding on to each other seemed uncomfortable for her. They merely skated at a leisurely pace around the rink with the rest of the group.

Still, he enjoyed holding on to her, watching her smile and mouth the words to the carols. It was more than enough.

"THAT WAS FUN," Bella said, as they left the rink and headed into town. She radiated happiness. It was the first time he'd seen her really beam since she'd arrived. The transformation was astounding. Her cheeks and nose were rosy from the cold, her hair had pushed back off her lovely face and her smile was infectious.

"What's been keeping you away from skating in Chicago? You seem to enjoy it, not to mention how good you are at it. Much better than me and I get on the ice every winter, mostly with my nephews."

"Time, I guess. I don't seem to have enough of it. I'm always working."

She fixed her hair around her face, but Travis liked seeing it all pulled back, making her appear less formal, less severe.

"We all need to take a break every now and then. Playing is good for us."

Travis was hoping she'd see what she'd been missing.

"I don't believe in breaks, at least not until everything I've started is finished."

"And I suppose that includes the sale of your dad's inn."

Her smile faded and Travis knew that was exactly the wrong thing to say.

"Yes. Thank you for reminding me. No more messing around. It's getting late and the roads look as if they've been plowed. My dad's probably on his way home by now. I need to get those new clothes and get back to the inn." She glanced at her watch. "I've got some phone calls to make before it gets too late."

Travis wanted to kick himself. All the ground he'd made with her had evaporated in a heartbeat. She had returned to her business mode and it didn't seem as if Travis would be able to get her out of it this time.

Unless...

"Not a problem. But before you start shopping, Holy Rollers makes some of the best hot chocolate and cookies around."

She hesitated.

Travis thought he had little chance of swaying her. But then she asked, "Do they have any of those fudgy chocolate cookies my dad used to make?"

Travis couldn't believe his luck. "As a matter of fact, they do."

She gazed at her watch again. "Okay, but only if we can stop in really quick."

He knew there was absolutely no way anyone could get in and out of Holy Rollers quickly, especially this time of year. The place was a nonending line.

"Sure, in and out. Not a problem."

"Then let's go."

BELLA HADN'T ALLOWED herself real hot chocolate and cookies in more years than she could remember. The combination of the two sent a sugar rush to her head that made for an almost euphoric experience. She couldn't seem to stop herself from smiling at everyone who walked into Holy Rollers, which caused everyone to smile back with a "Merry Christmas" greeting. She had no choice but to nod and repeat the politically incorrect salutation. She knew better. "Happy Holidays" had been her greeting of choice whenever she was forced into responding, but no one in this town seemed to be of the "holiday" politically correct mind. Christmas was king in Briggs, and if she ate any more cookies, no doubt the mayor would christen her the town's honorary greeter.

Holy Roller's bakery had proved to be everything a bakery should be...not that Chicago didn't have its share of bakeries. They did. Some of them were outstanding. But the charm that Holy Roller's exuded from the glass display cases filled with an assortment of muffins, cookies, cakes, tarts and donuts to the antique tables and chairs set up along the redbrick wall couldn't be surpassed in any big city.

Two hours later, as Bella took the last bite of her sixth fudgy cookie and scraped out the final bits of foam from the bottom of her second mug of hot cocoa, she sat back, completely content from her sugar high. Not only was she warmed by the atmosphere inside the bakery, but she was feeling more comfortable hanging out with Travis, despite his obsession for all things Christmas.

"Can I get you guys anything else?" Amanda asked. Bella instantly recognized her as Milo's wife, the pink-haired twenty-something pregnant girl who had sat in the back of the sleigh belting out Christmas carols. She hadn't paid much attention to her last night, not wanting to make friends with people she'd never see again, but Amanda was a true beauty with a friendly greeting for everyone who entered the bakery. She seemed like a traditional country girl, despite her bright pink, close-cropped hair. What Bella had noticed most was how protective Milo Gump, the bartender, had been of her. Milo had to weigh in around three hundred pounds to Amanda's one hundred, yet he was as gentle to her as a baby lamb with its mama.

Travis looked over at Bella and she could tell he was trying to decide if she needed yet another refill on her hot chocolate.

"I'm fine, thanks," she assured him and Amanda.

"I think we need a dozen of those fudgy cookies to go," Travis told Amanda.

Bella thought about arguing, but then decided cookies as a late-night snack would be perfect with a tall glass of cinnamon milk, a treat her dad prepared especially for her whenever she couldn't sleep. Something she hadn't thought of since her mom tried to recreate it in their tiny kitchen in Chicago soon after they'd first arrived. Her mom couldn't cook and had scorched the milk and added way too much cinnamon. It was awful, so Bella never asked for it again.

"Coming right up." She turned to Bella. "So how long are you in town for?"

"At least until tomorrow."

"Oh, you've got to stay until Christmas. That's the absolute best holiday in Briggs, especially this year with all the fun events planned. My husband, Milo...do you remember him?"

"He's not the kind of man anyone can easily forget."

Amanda beamed. "Yeah, I know. He's such a sweetie pie. We'll be attending almost everything. The one we're really looking forward to is the snow-sculpting contest out in front of your dad's inn. You should participate. It's such a hoot. Milo and I are carving a mini replica of the inn. We drew up the plans and everything. Your dad's going to love it."

The sugar high was fading, but looking into Amanda's innocent eyes, then glancing over at Travis, who gave her a look as if she was on her own for this one, she couldn't bring herself to tell the truth.

"I'm not much of an artist, but I'll be there. I can't wait to see how the snow inn turns out."

Amanda clapped her hands in quick succession, not really making any noise, just pressing her fingers together, while her face lit up with genuine joy. Bella wondered how someone could be that excited over a snow-sculpting contest. "Travis promised to carve something this year. Usually he only judges, but this year he made a promise. I'm sure you can help him."

She gazed over at Travis.

"Sure you can," he told Bella, grinning. "I'd love it."

Bella smiled up at Amanda. "I'll certainly try."

"Oh, you'll do fine, I'm sure."

Bella had stepped into it now. Not only had she agreed to stay until the contest, whenever that was, but she'd agreed to help carve out something corny, she was sure. Problem was, she had absolutely no intention of doing either one. Besides, all this good cheer and happiness was giving her a stomachache. Or was it the six cookies and refills of hot chocolate made with whole milk, no doubt.

She didn't know about her malady, but she did know she couldn't and shouldn't stay, no matter how much she secretly wanted to. The whole idea of hanging around until Christmas seemed truly delightful and it was something she'd thought about many times while she was growing up.

She gazed over at Travis, who seemed to be enjoying himself and decided she simply could not allow herself to get sucked into this small-town madness. The inn had to close and the guests had to leave before Christmas Eve. That was the agreement she'd made with her father and with TransGlobal. And she intended to keep it.

Just not right now.

Chapter Four

Not only did the town of Briggs, Idaho, look like a post-card for Christmas mania, it sounded like it, as well. Nat King Cole crooned his rendition of "Noel" as Bella and Travis exited Hess's Department Store. She'd done some major damage to her credit card, charging three new sweaters, two pairs of jeans, a pair of warm, waterproof gray boots which she wore out of the store, practical and not-so-practical lingerie, warm pajamas, several scarves, a knit hat, as well as four pairs of fuzzy socks and two pairs of gloves. The gloves came with a third pair adorned with Santa, Rudolph and elf heads sewn onto the tops of each finger, like minipuppets complete with tiny beads for eyes. She had tried to tell the perky sales girl that she didn't want or need the pup-pet gloves, but the girl wouldn't hear of it. No matter. Warm clothing was essential, and the puppet gloves were one hundred percent wool. Not that she would ever purposely wear them.

She could barely carry everything and if it wasn't for Travis offering to help, she wouldn't have been able to make it up the street.

Problem was she wasn't sure she wanted his help. It only perpetuated the problem she had being around him. The more time she spent with him the less anger she felt toward him and the more she wanted to feel his lips on hers…a thought that frightened her, especially now as they stood in front of her room at the inn.

"Thanks," she told him after she unlocked and opened her door. "I had a nice day."

"Me, too," he said, standing a little too close. "Where do you want these?"

She began taking the bags from him not wanting him to step one foot in her room, knowing that if he did, she would never want him to leave.

"I can take them," she told him.

"Not a problem."

He ignored her request and entered the cozy room. The four-poster bed, made up in a thick wine-colored quilt, dominated the room, causing her to fantasize about making love to this grown-up Travis. The thought of his naked body pressed up against hers prompted a hot flash to race through her with such intensity that she couldn't move away from the doorway.

"I'll just put these on the bed," he said.

"No! Not the bed."

Her voice startled him as he grabbed hold of the bags as if they might explode if he put them down.

"Okay, definitely not the bed. So where do you want them?"

She could feel the blush on her face. "The chair. Just put them on the chair."

He followed orders then turned and headed her way, smirking as if he knew exactly what she'd been thinking.

"Did you want to get some dinner? It's been a long day. You must be hungry." He stood no more than five inches from her and she wanted nothing more than to be wrapped in his strong arms.

She took a step closer to him, his hand brushing against hers, her pulse quickening.

"I'll grab something from my dad's fridge, but thanks for the offer."

He took a step in even closer. She could feel his warm breath on her face.

"Bella, look, I know we got off on the wrong foot. Maybe we can start all over again."

"It was a nice day, Travis. Thank you for that."

She waited for his kiss.

They were almost touching now. Her heart raced, and her warm clothes only enhanced the heat she felt prick her skin. She wanted out of her coat, and more importantly, she wanted out of her clothes.

"Anytime."

They stood staring at each other for a moment. A surge of emotion raced through her and she needed to tell him how she felt, how much she wanted him in her bed.

"Travis, I…"

But before she could finish her thought, he gently kissed her on the cheek, tickling her skin with his beard then he brushed past her and proceeded down the deserted hallway.

"See you in the morning," he called back to her, leaving her standing there wondering what the heck had just happened.

It HAD TAKEN every ounce of self-control that Travis could muster to walk away from Bella. Their day together had stirred up emotions, emotions that now took on a deeper meaning. She had grown into a stunning beauty with a smile that could light a spark under him on the darkest of days. Despite her orneriness, and her sometimes brash behavior, he now knew there was a completely wonderful side to Bella, a caring, loving side that he wanted to get to know all over again.

He was falling hard and fast for this grown-up Bella and he didn't know if he could stop his emotions now that he'd gotten a peek of the real woman she tried to keep hidden.

He'd always had a soft spot in his heart for her, but that was more of a child's crush. It was different now. The passions ran deeper. Maybe he couldn't call it love exactly; instead it felt like a longing in his soul. He knew if he was around her much longer he might end up on the wrong end of the branding iron, but he was willing to take the chance.

The thought scared him more than being caught up a tree with a grizzly on his tail.

This wasn't supposed to happen. The task Nick had set out for him was to reintroduce her to Briggs and everything she once loved, not to stir up his own intense feelings for her.

His saddle was slipping and there was only one person who could help him set it right again.

"Come right in, little brother. I've been expecting you," Colt said as he escorted Travis into his living room. "The kids are thankfully down for the night and Helen's catching up on her email in her office. Brandy? It's cold out there."

That was the thing about Colt. He seemed to have a sixth sense going on when it came to matters of the heart. He always knew exactly when his two brothers needed guidance and offered it willingly.

"The good stuff. Maybe it'll help 'cause right now I feel I ain't got nothin' under this ole hat but hair."

Travis plopped himself down on the cream-colored sofa in the living room. Colt took his coat while Travis slipped off his hat and set it down on the wooden coffee table, the table he'd crafted out of reclaimed wood from the family barn floor. An eight-foot spruce with colored lights and an assortment of ornaments anchored the room with Christmas cheer while garland, wooden nutcrackers and six empty stockings lined the mantel. A fire burned in the hearth warming Travis from the bitter cold night, giving him a shiver as he tried to settle his nerves, anticipating not only the brandy, but knowing Colt would provide the guidance he needed.

"That girl always was a fire under your skin," Colt said as he handed Travis a cocktail glass containing three fingers of brandy then took a seat in his favorite leather chair across from Travis. He moved the doll with the cowgirl hat and long braids and carefully sat her on top of a large toy box in the corner.

Even though curly-haired Loran was almost three years old, Travis still had a difficult time wrapping his head around the fact that Colt was daddy to a bubbly daughter. For the longest time it had been Colt and his three boys until his friend Helen, now his fetching wife, came up with a miracle baby and changed everything. And it was a good thing mama-fate had stepped in because Travis was sure his brother would have worked himself to death on the Granger family ranch to assuage his guilt over losing his first wife in childbirth.

Colt was now a contented dad and husband who had

learned how to temper his workload with family and friends.

"Daddy, I don't feel so good," Joey said when he walked into the living room, rubbing his eyes. "I think I'm going to throw up."

"Hold on there, little man," Colt said as he whisked Joey up in his arms and dashed down the hallway to the bathroom.

Not a minute later, Colt's middle son, Gavin, appeared. "My throat hurts, Uncle Travis, and I can't sleep."

And before Travis could react, little Loran staggered into the room. "I want my mommy. Where's my mommy?"

At once the entire house seemed to erupt with sick children, bright lights and adults trying their best to accommodate them. Helen, with her long red hair and can-do disposition simply appeared and whisked Loran up in her arms, trying to sooth her with sweet talk, gently moving her strawberry-colored curls off of her face.

Travis went into action along with Colt, trying his best to help Joey after he vomited all over himself, the floor and apparently his favorite robot.

"It's okay," Travis told him as he helped clean him up and slip on some clean pajamas.

"I didn't mean…to…throw up. Honest, I didn't," Joey said in between tears and hiccups.

"No worries. Even cowboys get sick every now and then."

"Do you…get sick, Uncle Travis?"

"All the time." But Travis had an iron stomach. It took a lot for him to feel any nausea. He figured he took after his dad. He couldn't remember Dodge ever getting sick.

Buddy, Colt's oldest, walked out of his room, joining the ruckus and looking about as tired as Travis felt. His baby face seemed to be changing by the minute, and along with his deep baritone voice, he was growing up faster than Travis could keep up with. "What's all the commotion?"

"Your siblings are sick," Travis told him, noticing Buddy's height. Except for maybe an inch or two, he was already almost as tall as Travis.

Buddy nodded, then yawned, pulling in a double dose of air.

"How do you feel?" Helen asked, her hand on his forehead feeling for a temperature.

Buddy answered, "Sleepy, but I'm okay."

"Go back to bed, sweetheart. You have a test tomorrow. You need your rest. We'll be fine." She gave him a hug and a reassuring kiss on the cheek. Helen was a good mother to Colt's boys and they loved her more than she probably knew because of it. Helen had come into the family when the boys were completely out of control, and within a few months she'd added discipline and structure to their lives, something Colt had been too busy with the ranch to see that they needed.

Buddy nodded and padded back to his room, his blue pajama legs dragging on the wooden floor.

For the next half hour the adults cuddled, comforted, administered various forms of children's meds, took temperatures, helped change pajamas and eventually tucked everyone back into their beds.

Helen climbed into bed next to Loran, who had demanded her mom sing her a lullaby, which Helen gladly delivered. Colt changed into his dark blue pajama bottoms, a loose-fitting black tee and a terry-cloth robe that he didn't bother to fasten. He plopped himself down in the recliner across from Travis as if nothing out of the usual had just transpired.

It was right then that moment when Travis began to realize what he really wanted: a family of his own. Problem was, there was only one woman he wanted and no way was that woman ready for a family of any kind.

Travis let out a sigh after he drank a good amount of the amber-colored elixir. It went down smooth and easy-like, warming his thoughts. He blew out the tension, sank into the wide sofa and rested his weary head against the inviting textured cloth.

"Sorry about all of that. They can be a real handful. But you have my full attention now. That beard of yours is growing fast. It must be driving you crazy."

Travis scratched his chin. Just mentioning his beard caused it to itch.

"It is. It's all Bella's fault."

"Ah, yes, the fire under your skin. How's that going so far?"

"She's turned into a blaze. I almost did something about it tonight."

"What stopped you?" Colt sipped on his brandy, looking as though he really enjoyed the taste, taking the time to swirl it in his mouth.

"She would have torn my heart out in the morning. It's her dang business deal with some company named TransGlobal."

"I take it that's the company buying Nick's inn."

"The very same."

"And you're against it because…?" He held his glass

in his lap, as if he didn't want the brandy to get too far away from him.

"You know exactly why I'm against it. That inn means everything to Nick." Travis slipped his legs out in front of him and crossed his ankles feeling much more comfortable. He'd removed his boots when he'd first sat down, and now he slipped off his belt. The fire crackled from the fresh logs he'd placed in the hearth, releasing the scent of burning hardwood, reminding him of winters past.

"Apparently not as much as it does to you."

The statement took Travis by surprise. "What are you getting at?"

"You're not here to talk about Dream Weaver Inn. It's Bella that's your problem. I think you need to keep those two heart pulls separate, little brother, or you'll drive yourself crazy."

"But they're tied together. If Nick agrees to the sale, Bella will pack up her emotions, slip on her city boots and drive right on out of this valley for good this time. As long as her father lives here there's always a chance she'll return. Without him, there's no draw. No reason for her to stop by."

Colt rubbed his day-old stubble, and sat forward as he finished off his brandy. He put the empty glass down on the small table next to him. "Then you'll have to convince her to stay, and if I know anything about women, it'll take more than sharing her bed…although I'm sure you're a stellar lover."

Travis smirked, lifting an eyebrow.

Colt snorted. "Don't get too full of yourself, little brother. I threw that out there to accommodate your monster ego."

"No bigger than yours."

"Believe me, after being married to two different women, trying to raise three boys on my own, and becoming father to a strong-willed girl, my ego has taken some strong hits. Every now and then I get a glimpse of what it used to be like when Helen and I have a date night. But between the riding school, the kids, the students and working around Helen's busy schedule I have little use for a bloated ego. Still, I wouldn't have it any other way. I'm a lucky man."

"Is that your advice? Kill my ego?"

"That may be impossible. However, I'm thinking you might be getting in your own way. Think more about what Bella needs rather than what you want."

Colt picked up his glass and realized it was empty, so he twirled it between his fingers. He smiled over at Travis, giving him some time to think about what he'd said. As if what he'd said was some kind of pearl of wisdom.

How the heck was he supposed to know what Bella "needed"? He knew exactly what she wanted—to sell the inn. Wasn't that also what she needed? Wasn't this deal all about money and power? Bella seemed to want both of those things. Correction...Bella seemed to "need" both of those things.

Travis sunk deeper into the sofa.

"Okay, you want to explain exactly what you mean? I seem to be dim-witted when it comes to Bella. Local women, I get, but Bella is a woman of a different breed."

Colt stood. "This is something you have to work out for yourself, little brother. 'Sides, it's late and I have an early day tomorrow. Feel free to spend the night right there on that sofa. If you had worked on this here house like you promised, instead of the inn, we'd have a guest bedroom for you to crash in. But until you figure out what you want, all I can offer you is this couch. There are blankets and pillows in the usual place in the hall closet."

"Thanks. The sofa's fine. Don't want to go back out there tonight."

"Good, 'cause I got enough to worry about right here inside this house. I don't need to be worrying about my baby brother driving on slippery roads."

"Glad I could give you some peace, but I'm still reeling 'round like a pup trying to find a soft spot to lie down in."

"That's 'cause you're thinking with your usual stubborn head rather than that big heart of yours."

Travis stood and the two men hugged. Colt said, "The tree lights are on a timer, so you don't have to worry about turning them off. Get some sleep. My kids get up by five, and as it is now, that's only six hours away. And don't stress. It'll all come together. Everything always looks better in the morning."

"If you say so."

"I do, and I'm your older brother so you need to listen up."

"I'll do my best."

And as he said it the lights on the tree went out and within the next moment Colt had disappeared into his bedroom, leaving Travis alone to watch the now dying fire and consider if he had even the slightest inkling of what high-tech, high-energy city girl Bella actually needed.

He scratched his chin thinking that the concept of knowing what she needed was like trying to lasso a mountain lion.

I NEED A CUP of hot milk with cinnamon, Bella thought as she rolled over for the umpteenth time in her big old, empty bed. The sweet drink used to put her right to sleep when she was a kid. Something she had thought of at Holy Rollers earlier that night and longed for it now. Normally, she stayed away from dairy, especially twice in one day, but these were desperate times and required desperate measures.

When she was a kid and couldn't sleep she'd sneak into her parents' room and nudge her dad awake. Her mom would only scold her and send her back to bed, but Daddy never seemed to mind her middle-of-the-night visits. They'd tiptoe out of the bedroom and into the kitchen where Bella would sit on one of the chairs, swinging her feet while Daddy would heat the milk.

What she loved the best about it was sometimes he'd tell her a story that would captivate her imagination.

What she needed now was some straight advice on her growing feelings for Travis Granger. She couldn't afford to be falling for him. Besides, he obviously wasn't feeling the same or he already had a girlfriend. What other reasons could there possibly be for his odd behavior that left her standing in front of her room, alone, when she'd purposely given off all the right signals?

The man couldn't possibly be that oblivious.

Bella grabbed the thick terry robe, slid her feet into the matching slippers and went downstairs to the private kitchen wishing with all her might that her dad wasn't off in another town. She didn't know who would be cooking while her dad was away, but she knew he or she probably wouldn't know anything about her special cinnamon milk.

As soon as she swung open the kitchen door she realized her wish had come true…her dad was busy with food prep. He wore a white bibbed apron, jeans, sneakers, a deep red flannel shirt and a warm smile. Christmas music softly played on the radio in the background.

She couldn't seem to get away from the darn stuff. Fortunately, it was growing on her.

"I thought you'd never come home."

"I just went for the day but got stuck there. Had a date with someone." He held up two eggs. "Hungry?"

She gazed up at the large black-rimmed clock that still hung over the six burner industrial type gas stove. It registered five-thirty-five. Hardly time for breakfast unless she was going out to milk some cows.

"What kind of date?" He had peaked her curiosity.

"A friend," he said quickly, as if he didn't want to talk about it. "Now what can I get you?"

She decided to let it go. "I really would love some of your hot cinnamon milk, and maybe a little advice."

His smile broadened. "The milk's simple, the advice might not be what you want to hear."

"I didn't ask the question yet."

"I'm your dad. I think I know what brought you down to this here kitchen so early in the morning."

"I couldn't sleep is all, and I thought some hot milk might help," Bella said, reverting to her childhood accent.

Nick poured whole organic milk from a bottle into a small pot.

If she ever drank milk, which was rare, she never drank whole milk. Didn't everyone drink nonfat like she did?

He finished pouring the milk then shoved the bottle back into the refrigerator.

"It's Travis that brought you down this morning. He's a force to be reckoned with."

She stiffened, not sure she wanted to tell her dad how she was feeling about Travis.

"He may be, but that's no concern of mine."

"I may not have spent a lot of time with you since you and your mama moved to the windy city, but I know that look. It's the same look you had when you were troubled by him as a girl."

She pulled a chair out and settled in it, willing to listen to anything he had to say about Travis as long as she could keep her emotions to herself.

She sighed. "He's a stubborn cowboy who's used to getting his own way."

"That he is. And if I'm reading you right, you're a stubborn city girl who's used to getting your own way. Between the two of you, there isn't anything that's gonna get resolved, unless one of you gives a little."

She watched her dad for a minute while he added the cinnamon and a dollop of maple syrup to the milk, then stirred. Steam rose up from the pot and permeated the air with that wonderful sweet scent that took her back to her childhood.

"Well, it won't be me. I intend to get my own way with this real-estate deal. That hasn't changed. Just because you're avoiding me and haven't signed the documents yet doesn't mean I'm any less determined to make this happen."

She couldn't admit she was unsure about everything in her life at the moment. Instead, she needed to put up a tough businesslike front or her entire world would begin to unravel.

"I can respect that. But we're talking about Travis now, not the sale."

"I merely want to make sure you understand that I haven't changed my mind. You promised that you'd sign the paperwork once you read it."

He pulled two old-fashioned thick mugs out of a cupboard and poured in the steaming milk. Bella's mouth watered in anticipation.

"I'm a man of my word."

"Have you read them yet?"

He walked over to the table and handed her a mug, then pulled out a chair and sat across from her.

"Why don't we enjoy our milk first? It'll go down a lot easier if we don't talk business right now."

"Dad, I—"

"Has he kissed you yet?"

She flinched just as she was about to take a sip of the steaming amber colored liquid and it spilled out on the wooden table. A table that bore the scars of decades of meal preparations. She instantly jumped up, grabbed a cloth from the counter and wiped up her mess.

"Did it burn you?" her dad asked as he took the towel from her to wipe his side of the table.

"No. I'm fine. Why did you say that?"

"Say what?"

She poured what was left in the pot into her cup, placed the pot on the wooden table and sat back down in her chair.

"Why did you ask if he'd kissed me?"

"Did he?"

"On the cheek, but I have a feeling that wasn't the kind of kiss you're talking about. It was sweet."

"That's it?"

"I don't want anything more," she lied and took a sip of the milk. It tasted every bit as good as she remembered it, smooth and rich, exactly how she liked it.

"Why not?"

"Because he broke my heart."

"Now how'd he do that? If any hearts were broken it most likely was his. You were the one who left, not him."

"Through no fault of my own."

She wrapped her hands around the cup and shuddered as the temperature from both the cup and the milk warmed her.

"I know you wanted to stay. But your place was with your mama. She wanted more for you than she had and I couldn't give it to you while we lived in Briggs. She was happy in Chicago. Are you?"

He blew on his milk then took several big gulps.

She joined him, deciding the temperature was perfect. Just warm enough to bring out the subtle flavors of cinnamon and maple.

"Of course I'm happy. How could I not be? I'm about to get an amazing promotion and move into my dream condo overlooking the lake. This deal alone will give me more money than I ever dreamed of making."

Repeating the reality calmed her.

"So you equate money with happiness?"

"No—not entirely—but it sure does make life easier if you have it. You've struggled your entire life with trying to make a go of this inn. Wouldn't you have been happier in Chicago with Mom and me running a profitable business?"

His brow furrowed. "I'm not cut out for the city. I'm a cowboy who just happens to run an inn. I need open sky and open range." He reached across the table and rested his hand on Bella's. All at once, his love swept over her. "I have a feeling you do, too. You can't tell me that you don't love this valley. Not when you loved it so much when you were growing up here. That kind of emotion for your hometown doesn't disappear."

"You don't know me anymore, Dad. I'm not that starry-eyed little girl who just about lived for my friends and Christmas fairy tales. I grew up, and sure this valley has some sentimental value, but I'm past caring about it. I've moved on and it's time you did, too."

Saying the words out loud caused her stomach to pitch.

"I can't believe that."

She looked down at her mug of steaming milk. It was beginning to lose its charm. "It's true. I don't care about Briggs or Christmas or Travis Granger."

The words caught in her throat.

"Yet here you are, and Amanda tells me you're joining in on the snow-sculpture contest tomorrow with Travis, the boy you say who broke your heart. Just how did he do that, again?"

She hesitated, not really sure she wanted to tell him. Thinking how it sounded so childish. "It's silly, I know, but to a young teen it was devastating. As soon as I left, he took up with the popular girls from school. The girls he always told me he disliked. Even now he seems to be the town stud."

"How do you figure?"

"I saw him at Belly Up, flirting with several women."

"Didn't mean nothing. He's dated a lot of girls in this town, and some from other towns. Never could settle on one, though. That boy's been in love with you ever since you two first met."

"He sure has a funny way of showing it."

"Might be true now that he's all grown up and a little full of himself, but he's one of the reasons why your mama took you away."

"What? I don't understand."

"She was afraid you'd end up like her if you stayed in this town."

"What does that mean?"

He paused, gazed down at the table, then back at Bella. "Your mama loved you like nothing else and only wanted what she thought was best for you."

"What are you trying to say, Dad?"

She slipped her hand out from under his.

"I don't want to disparage your mama, but she believed if you stayed in Briggs, you'd end up like she did. Pregnant when you were still a teen, stuck in a small town, married to a man you resented."

His words burned through her.

"What? That's why we left? I was twelve. Travis and I were just kids."

His eyes welled up. "I fell in love with your mama when we were kids, like you and Travis did. But your mama didn't share those same feelings."

"She loved you. She told me she did."

"At some point when we were young, maybe she did. As time went on, and life got more difficult, she didn't like being near me, and resented this inn. When she watched you carry on with Travis, she saw history repeating itself. Her own mama had done the same thing. She wanted to break the cycle."

"And you let her?"

"There was no stopping your mama once she put her mind to something."

Bella knew she had the same trait.

"Did my mom purposely not leave a forwarding address when we moved?"

"I don't know."

"Is that why I was only allowed to visit a couple of times, and she came with me? And you only came out to Chicago a handful of times?"

"Yes."

"And you let her get away with that?"

"She had sole custody. I didn't have a choice."

Tension gripped Bella's insides, causing the milk to sour in her stomach.

"Did you ever sue her for custody?"

"Sure did. I couldn't bear being that far away from you. I thought it would bring you both back to me, but all it did was make her more determined to take control."

"And you didn't continue to fight for me?"

"Not after that. No. I'm sorry I…"

He reached out for her as her eyes pooled with tears, but she couldn't be consoled. She pushed herself up from the table once again knocking over her mug, but this time she didn't stop to clean it up.

Chapter Five

Bella didn't go back to bed after her talk with her dad in the kitchen. Instead she dried her eyes on her rose-embossed hankie, pulled herself together and prepared for the day. Now that she knew the facts of her parents' divorce, she could continue on her mission. Even though it had broken her heart, her mom had been right in taking her out of this dead-end town and away from Travis and her dad. Neither one of them were worth any more of her concern. Her dad had given up the custody battle and Travis had moved on years ago. No way did he still love her. That was simply misguided thinking on her dad's part.

She'd been allowing Christmas nostalgia to sidle into her heart, thinking that her dad and Travis deserved the benefit of the doubt. Now that she knew their true character, she relocked the door to her heart, tighter this time, so nothing could seep inside.

If her dad didn't want to sign the agreed upon offer willingly, then she'd have to force his hand. They'd made a verbal agreement to have the inn closed by Christmas Eve, and Bella intended to see to it that he kept that commitment.

The first thing that had to be done was to inform the

guests that the inn would be closing and they'd have to find accommodations elsewhere. She called several local motels in the area, as well as in Jackson which was less than an hour away, and was able to secure several rooms at the same price the guests were paying at Dream Weaver Inn. The local motel owners were more than happy to have the business. The managers of the motels and inns in Jackson weren't as eager. They were almost booked solid and only had their higher-priced rooms available, but when she mentioned her dad's name and the Dream Weaver Inn, they were more than happy to accommodate.

She printed up the notices on the inn's official stationary and slipped them under each guest's door well before breakfast was served in the dining room. The relocation notices caused quite the uproar with the guests, her father, and—she assumed—Travis who was also informed by an official email from Dream Weaver Inn that his snow-sculpting contest would have to be moved to another location or cancelled. Personally, she didn't care what he decided to do with it, but the event would definitely not be sponsored by Dream Weaver Inn, nor would it take place on the inn's front lawn.

There was a knock on her room door, probably her dad asking her to reverse their plans. She took a deep breath to strengthen her resolve and opened the door.

"You can't do this," Travis blustered. He looked as adorable as ever in his black hat, low on his forehead, a black shirt and jeans that hugged his hips like they were tailored just for him.

She tried to ignore the constant attraction she couldn't seem to shake, no matter what she thought of his behavior. It was frustrating and the sooner this whole thing was over with the sooner she could go home and be rid of him once and for all.

"Coffee's still hot if you want a cup," she told him, pointing to the tray she'd brought up from the kitchen. The tray sat on a small round table in front of the windows, loaded down with a basket of muffins, an assortment of jams and jellies, honey, butter and the leftover fudgy cookies from Holy Rollers. "There's an extra mug on the dresser you can use. Go ahead and help yourself to a muffin or a cookie. The cookies seem to taste even better this morning."

She didn't want to get into it with Travis, thinking coffee and a muffin might soothe his obviously bruised ego.

"Dang it all, Bella, you have no right to cancel the snow-sculpting event one day before it's supposed to take place. I've got a truckload of clean snow arriving in two hours for the contestants. There are more than seventy-five people signed up for the event. They've already paid their entry fee, not to mention all the hours some of them have worked on their plans."

"I only did what my dad and I agreed upon," she told him, then sat down in front of her laptop. She was busy securing a reputable estate dealer who was free to come in and give her a price for all the furniture inside the inn. Something her dad had agreed to do, but hadn't. She intended to have all the details finalized by December twenty-third which gave her only four more days to get everything sorted out before her meeting on Christmas Eve with TransGlobal. The trip to Florida would have to wait until after Christmas.

"Unless your dad has signed those papers, and correct me if I'm wrong, even then he still owns the place until Escrow closes. You have no authority to do any of this."

"My dad and I have a verbal agreement. The law is on my side. We made that deal before I arrived and I'm simply implementing the terms. I have a recording of his acceptance on my phone."

Travis's eyes went wide. "You recorded a conversation between you and your father?"

"It's a good business practice."

"He's your father."

A loud thump echoed overhead and Travis glanced up but didn't mention it to Bella. She'd hired a company to remove everything in the attic. Her dad had taken out what he'd wanted and left everything else up there. She wanted nothing to do with any of that junk any longer.

"It's still business."

"Is that how business is done in Chicago?"

She turned to him shaking her head. "No. It's what I've learned since I've gotten burned a couple times."

His anger softened as he approached her. She could tell he was changing gears to use a different approach. She refused to be taken in by his charms once again. "Bella, this is Briggs. Nobody's going to *burn* you here."

"Oh? The possibility is very real." She wanted to tell him she'd already been scorched by her parents, but she let it slide…for now.

"You can't mean that. Besides, you told Amanda while we dined on your favorite cookies and hot cocoa that you would try your hand at snow sculpting. That couldn't have been a lie. I saw the truth on your face."

Footsteps clomped down the attic stairs and a few seconds later another set of footsteps stomped back up.

"What the heck is Nick doing up there?" Travis asked turning to face the door as if he was ready to check it out. She didn't want him involved so she went along with his illusion that it was Nick making all the noise and not the two guys from the company she'd hired to haul everything away.

"He's sorting out his things. Anyway, what you saw was a sugar high. It's worn off now. A lot has changed since yesterday."

"Tell me what's changed and I'll try to fix it." He took a couple steps closer to her. She stood and wanted to lash out at him about his decision to go along with her parents and not contact her. She wondered if he had any idea how much that hurt.

"Some things can't be fixed."

"There's always a way to make things right again."

"Right according to whom?"

"According to whatever it takes to change your mind about all of this. It's not only about the snow-sculpting contest, you're evicting your dad's guests only days before Christmas. Who does that?"

"I do, when it benefits my family."

More noise came from the attic, but this time Travis seemed to ignore it.

"Throwing your dad's valued customers out in the snow and cancelling something fun that this town has been anticipating is somehow beneficial to you and your family? Enlighten me, 'cause I'm blind as to how that works."

"I don't have to 'enlighten' you. It's my decision to make and I've made it. Besides, this is none of your business."

"Now see, that's where you're wrong. Since you're

trying to cancel one of my events that makes it my business. And I don't intend to let you get away with it. The snow-sculpting contest will go on as planned."

"Not on my father's property it won't, or I'll have the lot of you arrested for trespassing."

He leaned in, only a whisper away from her face, smiled and said, "Apparently you've forgotten how stubborn and resourceful I can be."

His breath smelled of candy canes and chocolate. Did he have to be so tempting? Nevertheless, she stood her ground, not wanting him to get the upper hand. "Don't test me."

He chuckled. "Is that supposed to scare me?"

"No. It's supposed to make you back off."

"Never going to happen."

"Then it should be an interesting couple of days."

By the time Travis got to the lobby he saw Miller's Moving & Storage van getting ready to pull away from the inn with what he quickly figured out was everything from the attic. At first, he was going to let it all go, but he reconsidered and ran out to stop them. He ended up saving a few of Bella's things, including the trunk, knowing darn well she was acting on pure meanness rather than any kind of reason. He'd hang on to everything for as long as she was in town in case she reconsidered. After that, he didn't know what he'd do with her things, but for now, he'd store them at his house.

Travis pulled out his phone and went into immediate action enlisting his family's help as he sat on the brown leather chair in the lobby watching as guest after guest checked out and received maps and instructions from Janet, the fifty-something woman behind the front desk, for their next night's lodging. Janet handled each one with her usual good-natured demeanor. She'd been working that desk for as long as Travis could remember, and seemed to enjoy dealing with people.

It tore at his heart to watch the guests leave with their luggage in tow after he and Nick had worked so hard to bring them in. A few of the guests had children who kept asking where they were going. The parents seemed miffed, but most of them took the time to gently explain the disruption to their confused children.

Travis could only speculate why Bella had done such an about-face since yesterday. He thought they were hitting it off, making strides to be friends. He had her laughing again, genuine belly laughs, and he knew she had loved being on the ice again, and the snowball fight... The day had been magical. He had felt it when he held her hand. They were connecting.

He wondered if her sudden change of heart might have had something to do with his not kissing her good-night? He could tell she had wanted him to, but that wouldn't have been enough for him. He wanted much more from Bella than a good-night kiss.

Still, could she seriously react with such vengeance over something as simple as a missed kiss?

Or maybe he'd said something to offend her? Got her riled over some innocent statement.

Or maybe she'd wanted him to spend the night, but he'd been so caught up in his own confusion that he hadn't seen the signs.

He couldn't be sure what went on in her pretty little head, but as soon as he had everything settled for the contest, he intended to come right out and ask her.

That or he'd kiss her and see if that softened her or-nery disposition.

On the other hand, a kiss might ignite a fire within him that he wouldn't be prepared to handle. The woman was hell-bent on ruining Christmas for everyone around her, and he wasn't about to jump on that wagon.

He called both his brothers and their wives who had a few great ideas about moving the contest to the town square or to the empty parking lot behind Ronald Reagan Elementary and High School, but when he spoke to his dad, everything came together.

"Seems to me nobody can keep you off that there empty lot next door to the inn. 'Specially 'cause we own it," Dodge said with a lilt to his voice.

"Since when do the Grangers own a plot of land in town?"

"Since Edith and me got hitched. That there empty lot's been hers since she was twenty-one and her daddy gave it to her as a present on her birthday. Never knew what to build on it, so it's been lying there empty ever since. Waitin' for you to come along with a problem, I 'spose."

His dad had married Edith Abernathy a little over two years ago, and the entire family had welcomed her with open arms. She was the best thing that could have happened to his aging father, and now it seemed she was the best thing that could have happened to Travis.

He couldn't believe his luck. "And she'd be okay with this? A lot of people will be tramping around on it."

"She's the one who offered it when your brother Blake told her what's been going on. You know how she likes to help you boys out whenever she can."

"Then I expect to see you two here carving snow tomorrow," Travis said into his phone.

"Believe me, we won't be missing it. Edith's got herself a plan to make a teddy bear. Even made a special tool to give the critter some fur."

"Can't wait to see it. Give her a kiss from me and tell her thanks."

"Any reason to kiss that woman is fine by me." He chuckled.

When Travis disconnected he let out a whoop, then did a little dance right there in the lobby of Dream Weaver Inn. Fortunately, there weren't any guests checking out or they'd get the wrong idea.

BELLA SPENT TWO hours at the front desk helping Janet relocate the guests, which had proven to be more of a challenge than Bella had anticipated, especially when the Dyson family approached the desk.

"But Mommy, Santa won't be able to find us if we leave," the little girl with the cherub face said as tears streamed down her little cheeks. It took every ounce of strength Bella had not to collapse and change her mind about sending the Dyson family to another inn, but in the long run, she was convinced it was for the best. At least that was what she told herself as Mr. Dyson picked up his distraught daughter to comfort her. She couldn't have been more than five years old, with dark brown locks and a face that would melt even the stodgiest heart.

But she wasn't going to melt Bella's heart, no matter how many tears she cried. It was as if Bella had taken a dose of "strong will" and nothing would deter her from her mission.

"Don't you worry, sweetheart," Janet reassured the little girl. "Santa can find you anywhere you go."

But the little girl was inconsolable, and she buried her head on her dad's shoulder.

"I'm sorry, but I don't have a choice in this matter," Bella lied. It wasn't as if she had set out to be dishonest to people that morning, but when they refused to listen to reason, she felt as though she had no other option.

"We had a main water pipe burst and our house flooded. We had hoped Dream Weaver Inn would be our home for the next couple of weeks," Mrs. Dyson said. "When we booked the room Mr. Biondi gave us a great price and assured us we could spend Christmas at the inn. Our daughter had her heart set on it. We even put up a small tree in our room. It's too much trouble to bring it with us, and the motel in Jackson said we couldn't have a live tree in our room because of fire codes."

"And they're right. I'm surprised my dad allowed you to do so in one of our rooms. I'm sure we don't have a fire permit for such a thing."

The little girl kept rubbing her eyes and moaning. Bella couldn't look at her. She knew exactly what she was feeling and could identify with her every tear. Still, those days were long gone and the little girl would do better in this world of hard knocks if she learned that lesson now. Her parents couldn't seem to get her to stop sobbing. If Bella's mom had been there, she would've given her a stern talking to, just like the one she gave Bella when they drove away from Briggs on Christmas Eve fifteen years ago.

"But, Mama, I don't want to leave. Daddy will be all alone for Christmas, and Travis and me are exchang-

ing gifts," Bella said as she twisted herself in her seat to watch Briggs shrink in the distance.

"You mind me, young lady and stop your crying. You'll thank me one day for getting you out of this pathetic little town."

"No, Mama. I want to go back. Can we please go back?"

Her mom stopped the car on the side of the highway and turned to her. "We are not going back. Not now. Not ever. Our new home is in Chicago. I have a job that will pay me good money, and I intend to take it. I'm sorry this is so tough on you. It's tough on me, too. But as you get older and see all the opportunities that are in front of you, you'll thank me. Now wipe those tears away, and face the front of the car. We're moving forward, not backward." She handed Bella a rose-embossed hankie that had once belonged to her mom. Bella sucked up her emotions, wiped the tears off her cheeks, and shoved the hankie in her pocket. She never let her mom see her cry again.

Bella had used that hankie that very morning to remind herself to toughen up.

"Where is Mr. Biondi? I'd like to speak to him before we close our bill," Mr. Dyson said.

Bella had no idea where her dad had disappeared to. Ever since their talk that morning he'd been MIA. At first she assumed he must be running errands somewhere, and would return before noon, but it was going on one o'clock and he was nowhere to be found.

"You can find Mr. Biondi right out that side door," Travis said, pointing to the EXIT sign over the oak door next to the stairway. "He's building a snow family out on the front lawn. I think he's getting ready for the sculpting contest tomorrow."

Bella had a hard time believing that with everything going on, her dad would choose snowman building rather than dealing with his inn. Travis was simply pulling her chain. Her dad wasn't really out there.

"Maybe if we can speak to Mr. Biondi he might change his mind," Mrs. Dyson said and proceeded to walk toward the side door with Mr. Dyson and their daughter following close behind.

"I can assure you he's not out there, and even if he is, there's nothing he can do to change the situation." She was almost shouting as the Dysons disappeared out the side door.

She turned to Travis who was rubbing his chin. "I don't understand why he wouldn't listen to me. My dad wouldn't be wasting his time playing in the snow. If I know my dad, he's probably driving around town making sure his guests are settled in their new rooms. He's all about his guests."

"Actually, at the moment, he's all about building a family."

Bella looked where he pointed out the side window behind her and sure enough, there was her dad, a mini-chainsaw in hand, at least six children and a couple of adults watching as he sculpted a snowman the likes of which she had never seen before. It stood about six feet high, was soundly formed and entirely made out of packed snow. Even his top hat had been carved out of snow. It was pretty incredible, but that was beside the point.

Bella turned back to Travis knowing full well he was getting a kick out of watching the turn of events.

He leaned on the front desk, a great big smirk on his oh-so-adorable face, staring at her as if he had nothing better to do with his time.

"Don't you have somewhere to be?"

"Nope."

"Shouldn't you be finding a place to hold your silly contest?"

"Don't need to. Already found a new place."

"Isn't there some prep work you need to do? Like maybe collect some tools or something?"

"The contestants provide their own equipment. All I need to do is provide the snow." He did a mock yawn. "Until the snow arrives, I've got nothing to do but wait. Besides, this is much more fun."

He gestured toward four more guests approaching the front desk, looking every bit as angry as the previous couple.

Janet greeted them with pleasantries, but they weren't biting.

Bella braced herself for the onslaught, while Travis chuckled and stepped away from the desk.

"I don't think this is going to work," Nick said as Travis tended to his horses in the Dream Weaver corral, a wide wooden building with two rows of stalls with a generous aisle in between. Rio and Wildfire had been out in the small pasture for most of the day and Travis had only recently brought them back inside.

At one point every stall in the massive corral had been occupied by townsfolk who didn't want to give up their steed. Now it was empty except for the two Clydesdales that Travis boarded for several weeks during the winter. The kids loved these majestic creatures and Travis had no problem parading them around town pulling his sleigh. Unfortunately, that would have to wait until tomorrow night. Right now he needed to get them groomed and back in their stalls for the night.

He had a date.

"We can't give up yet," Travis told him.

"I've run out of ideas." Nick leaned against the open gate while Travis brushed the regal stallion with a curry comb.

"Well, I haven't."

"She's evicted all of my guests. My heart broke for the Dysons' little girl, but I couldn't do a thing about it. My hands are tied, Travis. Am I stupid for wanting to pass up this deal? She might be right. I could have a pretty nice life if I accept her offer."

Travis stopped combing his horse. "Doing what? Golfing?"

"There are worse ways to go through retirement."

"Personally, short of some debilitating disease, I can't think of one."

Nick started pacing in front of the stall, his boots making crunching sounds on the frozen dirt and straw.

"I've never been good with money, son, one of the reasons why her mom divorced me. I can't seem to make enough of it most of the time, then when I do I can't hold on to it. I tend to work with my emotions rather than any sense of logic. Bella's all about logic and maybe it's time for me to become more like her."

Travis stepped in front of him, so he could look into his eyes. "Nick, tell me one thing. Do you think your daughter's happy?"

"She told me she is and I'm thinking it might be time to take her at her word."

"I don't agree. I think she's torn up inside and it's our job to show her all that she'll gain if she stays put awhile."

Nick smirked. "And how's that working out for you so far?"

"Not so good, but I'm still optimistic, especially after yesterday. I saw the smile on her face like she was enjoying herself. If we can get more of those smiles and laughter—"

"She laughed?"

"Yep, when we were ice-skating."

"I'd like to see that."

"Give me another day, just one more day and I'll have her laughing so hard she'll be crying."

"And just how are you going to do that?"

Travis had no idea, but he wasn't about to admit that failure to Nick. "I've got me a foolproof plan."

Nick shook his head. "I think you're trying to pull the wool over my eyes. If I could see Bella laugh like that again, I'd pay you anything you wanted."

"No need. Just bake her several dozen of your fudgy cookies and put them in her room. That's our inroad with Bella. She loves those dang things and the sugar makes her giddy."

"I'll get right on it," Nick said. "Anything to get your plan in motion."

And they headed out of the corral. Now all Travis had to do was come up with another plan. Simple, if Bella wasn't so dang skeptical to everything he came up with. It seemed that so far, all the progress he'd made had slipped away. She was back to acting like the girl he didn't much like and if he couldn't get her to change her stripes fairly soon, he'd have to give up on her once and for all.

TWO HOURS LATER, about the time that Travis began to get itchy waiting for his snow to arrive, a long green flatbed truck backed up the driveway. The truck was piled high with clean snow. Another green truck idled curbside waiting for the first truck to dump its load. Two men jumped out of the second truck and proceeded to direct the driver of the first truck where to dump the snow.

Bella caught the movement outside through the window and stopped whatever she was doing behind the desk to direct her bitterness of everything fun towards Travis. He'd moved over to his favorite leather chair in the lobby after he'd turned on the Christmas-tree lights for the third time. Apparently, every time he left the room, someone, most likely Bella, turned them off.

"What's that load of snow doing out front? I thought you said you found another place for the contest?"

"Don't worry your Scroogey little self over my snow. They won't unload unless I tell them to." He said it with complete confidence and just as his statement settled in the air, the back of the truck began to pitch. Travis ran out the front door yelling and waving his hands for the driver to stop. Bella followed close behind, yelling her threats at Travis.

"You cannot unload that snow on this property. Tell them they have to stop," she shouted, but he ignored her trying instead to get the driver's attention.

In the meantime, another man, wearing a red-check flannel shirt, black jeans, heavy black boots and a red Santa hat approached Travis.

"Travis Granger?"

"That's me. Please tell your driver to hold on. That's not where I want the snow dumped. I phoned your office and told them we have ourselves a different location."

Another man showed up, a shorter, thinner version of the other wearing plastic elf ears, a green flannel shirt, green pants and black elf shoes. He spoke to someone on a two-way radio and the truck bed stopped in mid-air, tilted up at a forty-five-degree angle.

"That snow," Bella warned, as she kept walking toward the truck, "can't be dumped on this property."

"Merry Christmas, ma'am," the Santa-hat guy said, giving her a great big warm smile, showing off his pearly whites. He seemed like a happy kind of guy, with a big belly, a full white beard and a jovial nature. Travis speculated if, after he delivered the snow, he'd be playing Santa in some department store, or in the children's wing of the local hospital. He looked like the perfect Santa Claus.

Bella didn't respond to his cheerfulness; instead she kept approaching the truck.

"Don't mind her. She's practicing her Scrooge role for the play tomorrow night in the town square."

"I thought Scrooge was a man," the elf guy said.

"We're updating it to make it our own. A more modern version," Travis told him, smiling at the thought of seeing Bella onstage playing mean ole Scrooge. With her recent disposition, it wouldn't be much of a stretch. "You can dump the snow on the empty lot next door. If you drive right up on the land there's plenty of room toward the back fence."

The Santa guy held out a tablet and handed it to Travis. Travis signed his name and the two men walked back to the truck, with the elf guy saying something into his two-way radio. Then, as if the entire scene had been scripted for a movie, the truck bed pitched up again as the snow in the truck bed began sliding down. It continued just as Bella proceeded to walk around the back of the truck.

"Look out!" Travis yelled, but it was too late. Before Bella could react, the load of snow had begun slipping off the back of the high truck bed right in her path.

Travis ran at full speed toward Bella, grabbed her around the waist and pulled her in tight. Then with sheer force on his part, the two of them tumbled out of the way of the falling snow and landed under a bush with Bella on top of him. Her arms were around his neck, her cheek against his and her full body pressed tight against his.

"Are you all right? You near about scared me to an early grave," Travis said, as she squirmed on top of him.

"Certainly I'm all right. I would have been fine if you hadn't grabbed me like that. You could've killed me."

"I just saved your life, and that's how you're going to react?"

She rolled off of him, and tried to get up, but then fell back on the snow. She looked almost comical.

Travis leaned over her, abruptly serious. "Baby, are you all right? Did you break something? Are you dizzy? Should I call an ambulance?"

She laughed. "You should see the look on your face. If I didn't know better, I'd say you were genuinely concerned about my wellbeing."

"What the heck does that mean? Obviously I'm concerned. I couldn't handle it if anything happened to you."

"You're serious, aren't you?"

"Damn straight I'm serious."

And he kissed her. Right there in the snow, under the mulberry bush he'd helped Nick plant two summers ago.

Chapter Six

Having a truckload of snow almost come tumbling down on a person's body might give that person a reason to act irrationally. Might cause them momentary blindness, rash behavior, or at the very least, it might prompt them to do something that they couldn't undo.

Kissing Travis Granger was one of those moments. It wouldn't have been so bad had Bella not kissed him back, not touched his tongue with hers, not moaned when his kiss grew deeper, and certainly not kissed him again when he tried to move away from her. She would have been able to face him had she not done all of that.

But she had.

Not to mention her reaction to said kiss. Not only did she cry like a baby, but she ran from the scene before Travis had a chance to utter one word. Then she locked herself in her room and contemplated packing her bag and driving away without the signed paperwork she needed to close the biggest real-estate deal of her career.

All because of a simple kiss.

Not that his kiss was the least bit simple. It more or less fell into the realm of intoxicating and delicious, which she had always known it would be from the second she saw him dangling from the inn's roof strapped in that stupid harness. Travis, the boy, would cause her toes to curl, and Travis, the man, made her want to curl up next to him in a bed somewhere for the next week or month or year.

The entire incident gave her a headache, and if she kissed him again—a thought that made her heart race— he could get her to do anything, including giving up the real-estate deal.

Four hours, three cups of cold coffee and one dozen fudgy cookies later she was ready to face the day, and the remainder of the disgruntled occupants of the inn according to Janet, everyone had relocated except the occupant of room two-ten which was assigned to Travis Granger. Apparently, he liked to stay in town as Christmas approached and her dad's inn had always been his first choice.

She'd given him an eviction notice that morning along with everyone else, but the man had a stubborn streak as wide as Nebraska and refused to leave even after Janet had tried to convince him it was for the best.

"He simply won't go," Janet told Bella on the room phone.

"Did you tell him he has no choice?"

"Yes, ma'am, but he insists that he's not going anywhere until the front door is locked and Nick drives away. I don't know what else to do."

"I'll take care of it. You've been a huge help and did more than your share today. You can go home if you want to."

"I've got another couple of hours to go on my shift and there's still some paperwork I'd like to finish before I leave, if that's all right with you." She sounded sincere and a little emotional, but Bella refused to let it get to her.

"Do what you think is best."

"Thank you, ma'am. Will you be coming down soon?"

"I'll be up in room two-ten trying to get Travis Granger to vacate the premises."

Janet chuckled. "Good luck with that, ma'am. He can be a bit mule-headed like the rest of those Grangers. Are you sure you don't want me to come along with you?"

Bella knew that Janet would be great at smoothing over things with Travis, but this was something Bella had to face on her own. Travis had to be dealt with no matter how much she dreaded seeing him again.

"Thanks, but I'll be fine."

Janet chuckled again, said her farewells and disconnected, leaving Bella with the ominous task. She squared her shoulders, took a deep breath, opened the door to her room and proceeded down the hall to face a man she both disliked and loved all at the same time.

TRAVIS KNEW BELLA would eventually come to his room to ask him to leave the inn, but fortunately his dad had stopped by since he was in town and his very presence had derailed Bella in her eviction-happy tracks. She'd tried several times to tell Travis to please vacate the premises, and each time Dodge had brought the conversation back around to his dinner invitation for Bella and Nick.

He was the master of avoidance when it suited him to do so, and Bella's eviction notice apparently was one of those times.

"I don't see how that's possible, Dodge," Bella told

him while still standing in the doorway looking amazing in one of the outfits she'd bought the night before. Her face glowed like a new moon on a cloudless night, and her hair looked like black silk. He wondered if it still smelled sweet like it had out in the snow. "My dad and I still have a lot to do to get ready to close this place down in the next couple of days."

Dodge had told Travis that he'd come into town to pick up a present for his wife, Edith, and decided to stop in at the inn to see what was happening. Then Travis had convinced him to invite Nick and Bella over to the main house for dinner. The way he had it worked out, a home-cooked meal might be exactly what Bella needed.

"Well, don't stand out in the hallway. Come on inside. Travis here has the fireplace going," Dodge urged.

There were a few rooms at the inn that came equipped with a gas fireplace, and his room happened to be one of them. As he watched Bella step inside, Travis was mighty pleased he'd settled on this room instead of a smaller one down the hall. The fireplace now acted as her lure.

She strode inside and Dodge closed the door behind her. The room was more of a suite than merely a bedroom. An antique mahogany desk sat in the corner with a matching mahogany chair, and a loveseat and an armless chair lived in front of the three windows that overlooked the street. The fireplace burned a bright range of reds, blues and whites on the far wall, while the king-size four-poster bed—that had already been made up by what was left of the staff—sat across from it.

Bella stood in front of the bed while Dodge stood next to her, and Travis sat on the desk chair. He'd been answering some email and taking care of ranch business. A small decorated tree sat on the desk complete with a bright shining star perched on the very top. From Bella's reaction to the Dyson family tree, he guessed she must be seething on the inside over his tabletop Christmas spruce.

As he watched Bella's arms fold across her ample chest, he wasn't so sure even Dodge could help out here. Bella seemed determined to destroy any scrap of Christmas cheer that might still remain somewhere in her memory.

"If you're packin' and workin' hard it's all the more reason for a good hearty meal. You look positively pale from lack of good home cookin'. If I remember right, your mama, God rest her weary soul, never was one for cookin'. Unless she changed her nature over the years, I bet you ain't had somethin' that can stick to your ribs since you and she done left this here town."

Dodge liked to appeal to a person's stomach more than his or her mind. He insisted that once a person had a full belly, he or she was more likely to agree to just about anything you proposed. Travis hoped that philosophy would work with Bella who seemed impervious to bribery of any kind.

Until now.

She smiled and her arms fell to her sides.

"I do remember that you made the absolute best chicken and waffles I've ever tasted. I've tried to make that meal myself and it didn't compare. I've even tried them at a couple restaurants and they never matched up. If you're inviting me over for your chicken and waffles you've got yourself a dinner guest."

Travis felt suddenly hopeful. His dad loved to get a request for one of his specialties, and he did, in fact, make the best chicken and waffles this side of the Rockies.

"For you I'll even pick up a fresh chicken from the organic chicken farm on up the road and make sure the griddle is extra hot to make them waffles crispy."

Her face lit up. "Will seven-thirty be all right?"

"It couldn't be better if I'd picked that time myself."

"I can drive you over," Travis said, his enthusiasm clear in his voice.

She turned to him. "Thanks, but I can drive myself."

"Then I should catch a ride with you. The main road in has been closed since the blizzard, so it might be tricky finding the alternate road. You'll need me to show you the best route."

"I have GPS on my phone."

"It doesn't work on these back roads."

"He's right," Dodge said. "There's already been three rescues this season 'cause of those dang GPS routes takin' folks out on roads that don't get you nowhere. I'd feel a whole lot better knowin' my son was leadin' the charge instead of some misguided beam shootin' down from a satellite in space."

Travis could tell by her temporary silence that she wanted no part of it, but if he knew this new Bella, logic would dictate her response and not emotions.

"Fine. You can hitch a ride there. But you're on your own getting home. I don't want to get stuck on some private Granger road."

Travis smirked. "I'll be coming right back here."

"Dream Weaver Inn is officially closed. You can't stay here."

"Until Nick throws me out, I'm staying put."

"Don't you have your own house to go to?"

"Sure do and I'd love for you to see it sometime. Thing is, this time of year, there's too much going on in town so I always stay at the inn. Besides, it's too much trouble to bring my sleigh home when I'll be needing it during the next couple of days."

"You have your horses boarded in our corral?"

He nodded and smiled. "Only place left in town and the boys are enjoying the change of scenery."

"You're exasperating."

"He's been called worse," Dodge piped in.

"Is that what you felt out in the snow today?" Travis asked, stepping in closer, almost whispering his words so Dodge wouldn't hear.

They stared at each other for a moment. That kiss still lingered on his lips and he knew she was thinking the same thing.

"I didn't feel anything. It was merely a kiss."

Dodge turned to Travis. "Maybe I should leave."

"No. Please, Dodge. Stay. I was just going," Bella said still looking all riled up. She turned to Travis. "Be ready at seven. I don't do late."

He saluted. "Yes, ma'am."

He caught the smile prick her lips, but she stifled it and spoke to Dodge. "Thanks for inviting my dad and me, Dodge. I'm looking forward to this evening. Now if you'll excuse me I have some business to attend to in my room."

And she walked away with Travis watching her leave. She always did have a fabulous walk: hips shifting with each step. He was enjoying the scene when his dad interrupted his appreciation.

"You owe me, son," he said. "That's one fine woman and if for some stroke of luck on your part, you're able to catch her love, never take her for granted or she'll fly the coop faster than a bull can throw a rider."

"I don't think I'll have to worry about that, Dad. She hates me."

"Only when you're tryin' to tell her what to do. Didn't you learn nothin' from your brothers and me? A woman don't need no man to tell her what she already knows."

"Then what does she need a man for?"

"Son, you're too old to be asking me that kind of loaded question."

"You know what I mean."

"I know it's time for me to get going if I'm puttin' on a dinner tonight." He grabbed his son's shoulder and Travis could feel the warmth emanating from his father's touch. "A man's gotta figure these things out for himself. I only hope you don't take too long with the figurin' 'cause that there filly's got her mind made up, and right now it don't include you."

BELLA HAD DRIVEN almost the entire route over to the Granger ranch in silence, listening to her dad and Travis chitchat about everything from the weather to Milo Gump playing Santa in the town-square gazebo tomorrow night.

She'd actually like to see that, if she could do it without Travis knowing about it. If he found out, she was sure he'd think she was softening her attitude towards Christmas and she most certainly was not. She was simply curious to see if Milo made an authentic looking Santa.

Her father still refused to sign the documents even though she'd taken all the necessary steps to empty out the inn. And if he stalled much longer, she would simply have no choice but to insist.

After all, it was for his own good. Her dad never could grab the gold ring when it was right in front of him. He always seemed to opt for the brass ring and it never brought him anything but tough times and heartache. Her mom had always been right about her dad. It was Bella she had misunderstood.

"You can pull up here," Travis said, yanking her out of her private thoughts.

The full moon combined with all the white Christmas lights that were strung from every surface and tree made her feel as though she'd just stepped into a Christmas card.

"The place is bigger than I remember it," she said as she beeped her truck locked and headed toward the Granger ranch house.

"My brother Doc Blake added on his dental office, and his wife, Maggie, added on her offices last year."

"They both work from home? Don't they get tired of each other?"

Bella couldn't imagine what it would be like to spend that much time with the same person every day, no matter how much you might love them.

Travis threw her an odd look as they walked up the front wooden steps with Nick following close behind. "Those two are as thick as feathers in a pillow. Plus, ever since Dodge moved on up the road, and they lost their babysitter, it makes it easier for them to take care of their kids. And now that there's another one on the way, Maggie loves the fact that she doesn't have to get into a car in the snow to get to her job. All she has to do is walk down the stairs and work in her pajamas if she's so inclined. It's about as perfect as red paint on a barn."

The front door opened and a rush of boisterous children, barking dogs and adults trying to keep the kids and dogs from overpowering the guests greeted them.

Fortunately the dogs didn't jump up on Bella or she'd have to turn around and leave. Dogs scared her ever since a crazed Chihuahua, that looked more like a rat with legs than a dog, bit her ankle.

"Uncle Travis. Uncle Travis. Is this the girl? The one who threw the snowball at me in town?" a young girl asked. She wore cowgirl boots, a lavender skirt and a pink cotton sweater. Her strawberry blond hair was pulled back in a long ponytail, and she had a sly little grin on her young face. She couldn't have been more than seven or eight years old, but Bella couldn't be sure. She was never good with guessing a child's age.

"Yes, Scout, this is Bella Biondi, Nick's daughter."

Scout looked up at her as she took her hand and guided her to the open doorway. "You sure can throw a snowball. We've been talking about it ever since you hit my cousin on the noggin. Nobody ever lands a snowball on Gavin. He's too quick. How'd you do that?"

An immediate rush of concern flowed over Bella. She had no idea she'd actually made contact with one of her snowballs. She'd simply lobbed them over to the group without aiming at anyone.

"I didn't realize I—"

"Yeah, you're the best shot we ever saw. Better than Uncle Travis or my dad or even Uncle Blake," a young boy said. He looked a lot like a miniature Colt.

"Are you Gavin?" Bella asked.

He nodded.

"I hope I didn't hurt you. If I did, I'm so sorry. I didn't—"

Another boy came up to her, and this one she recognized from the first day when she'd arrived, Colt's son, Joey. "It would take a lot more than a snowball to hurt Gavin. He's made out of steel. Besides, he's been chompin' at the bit waiting for you to get here so you can show him how to throw like that."

"C'mon, guys, give her a break," Colt said, making himself known. "She hasn't even gotten inside yet and you're pouncing on her with questions. Let's get her warmed up first."

An older woman put her arm around Bella. Normally, Bella would have tensed up and moved away from the woman's touch. She tended not to like overly friendly people, but she welcomed this woman's heartfelt warmth and moved in closer to her as she guided Bella through the wide doorway. "Sweetheart, I've got some mulled cider on the stove and a brand new bottle of brandy just waitin' to spread some Christmas cheer. I got a feeling you'd like nothing better than a warm mug right about now."

The kids continued to make a fuss over Travis, hanging all over him and roughhousing him as best they could, with what looked like the oldest of them swiping his hat and placing it on his own head. Travis seemed to love all the attention, and gave it right back to them, grabbing the smallest girl and flinging her up on his shoulders. She giggled with delight as she wrapped her arms around his neck.

Nick cut a path through the throng as an attractive woman in her fifties, Bella guessed, walked out on the porch and stood next to her dad and whispered something in his ear. He chuckled, then they turned away from everyone and went inside. Bella had never seen her before. She was about as tall as her dad, with dark shoulder-length hair, and a pretty, feminine face, as if she was once a model in her youth. She wore trendy clothes, a bit too trendy for Briggs, and seemed to carry herself with all the confidence of royalty. Bella attempted to follow them inside, but the older woman who had offered the cider curtailed Bella's movements.

"I'm Edith, Dodge's wife," the woman said over the squeals of laughter. "It's a pleasure to finally meet you. And that woman with your dad is Audrey. I'm sure he'll introduce you later, but right now let's get you inside where it's warm."

Too many names and references were coming at Bella at once, especially the part about "that woman with your dad." Bella had no idea what Edith was referring to. Her dad wasn't dating anyone. At least he hadn't mentioned it.

"Thanks," Bella told her as she stepped to one side of the barking dogs and squealing children. She loved watching Travis interact with kids. He obviously understood them and enjoyed their company. She knew one day he'd make a fabulous daddy. Unlike Bella who never really thought about having children of her own. Ever since she started climbing the corporate ladder, children didn't seem to have a place in her world.

"Hot cider would be perfect," Bella told Edith, while thinking how agreeing to this dinner was possibly the biggest mistake she'd made since she arrived in Briggs. Already she felt the tug of family, and home and Christmas pulling at her heart. And it didn't help that everyone was so friendly, and the house not only felt comfortable, but it hadn't changed much since the last time she'd seen it, only a day before she and her mom had driven away from everything she'd known and loved.

Once inside, Travis helped her out of her coat. She felt his fingers brush the back of her neck, and goose bumps instantly prickled her skin. The attraction she felt toward Travis was growing by leaps and bounds and no matter how hard she tried to ignore it or pretend she had her emotions under control, the man was once again taking hold of her heart and this time she might not be able to make him let go.

THE EVENING HAD gone exactly as Travis had hoped it would and by the time the pies were served, Bella seemed more relaxed than he'd ever seen her. She looked stunning with her hair pulled back off her face. Her eyes sparkled with each chuckle. He felt as if he was finally seeing the real Bella. He'd had a glimpse or two of this relaxed behavior while they were skating, but nothing this prolonged. It only made his longing for her more intense.

He was hoping this dinner, being part of his family, might be the tipping point she needed to cause her to reconsider selling the inn and maybe staying for a while, at least until Christmas.

"Do you remember when you and Travis decorated that there little pine tree out back?" Dodge asked Bella after he mixed cream into his mug of coffee.

Bella smiled and nodded. "We swiped all the ornaments off your tree in the living room and decorated our tree. I remember thinking how sad it looked compared to all the big trees out back, like it didn't belong. We decided the ornaments might make it feel happy."

"Don't forget the lights," Travis added. "We took those, too, and the garland, and the tree skirt and everything else we could find including some presents. We ran every extension cord we could find out the back door to that little tree. It lit up like a beacon."

"I'd just seen Charlie Brown Christmas and the tree out back looked exactly like his tree."

Edith busied herself with slicing the homemade pies and plating them: cherry, apple, pumpkin and pecan, which just happened to be Travis's favorite. A half-gallon container of Moo's vanilla-bean ice cream sat on the table next to the pies, along with a bowl of freshly whipped cream. Audrey helped serve the pies as Bella seemed to be watching her every move.

Travis had the feeling Bella wasn't too fond of Audrey and wanted to know more about her, but if he knew Nick, he wasn't talking. Nick was the kind of guy who kept his private life close to the vest, and any information about Audrey, he kept even closer. Travis had known Nick was courting a woman in Jackson for several years, but this was only the second time he'd met her. The first time was a few months ago at the annual fair, and that was just in passing. Inviting her to a family dinner at the Grangers meant the relationship had taken a serious turn. Only thing was, Nick might be moving to Florida in a few days. How was that going to work?

"That was the year Mom insisted we open some of our presents outside in the snow on Christmas Eve," Colt said.

"Sounds cold," Blake's wife, Maggie, said as she scooped out ice cream for the kids who didn't want pie.

"It was, but Mom kept us warm with hot chocolate and cider while Dad brought out lawn chairs and blankets to keep us comfy," Blake explained, smiling at the memory.

"Dad and Blake cleared the snow away and made a bonfire," Colt added. "One of their best, as I recall."

Travis turned to Bella. "Mom had insisted that if we had gone to all the trouble of stripping down the living-room tree to decorate the one out back, then by golly, we were going to celebrate Christmas Eve out by that little tree."

Audrey put down a large piece of pecan pie with an extra scoop of vanilla ice cream in front of Travis. He couldn't wait to dig in. Edith's pecan pie was just about the best pie he'd ever tasted.

"But all the trees out back are taller than this house," Joey countered. "What happened to the little tree?"

"It grew up," Bella said, with a touch of disdain to her voice. It was the first time all evening that Bella had snapped at anyone.

And just as she said it, Travis realized that back then—the very next day, on Christmas Eve, while his family was sitting outside in the cold enjoying Bella's pretty tree, she and her mom were on the road, heading for Chicago. He glanced over at her and saw the tears in her eyes.

Travis reached out across the table, but she pulled away faster than a jackrabbit running down a hole. "Bella, I—"

"Can we have Christmas Eve outside in the snow this year?" Scout asked.

Bella stood. "It's getting late and I have a lot to do in the morning. Thanks so much for inviting me, Dodge, Edith."

Everyone immediately begged her to stay, but Bella

was persistent. "Thanks, but I'm sorry, I can't—" her voice hitched. She turned to Nick. "Dad?"

He looked over at her like a deer in the headlights until Colt came to his rescue.

"No need to rush off, Nick. I can drive you home later."

Nick stood. "Thanks, but I best be leaving with my daughter."

Bella stopped him. "You can stay, Dad. That's finc. I just need to get going."

"Are you sure?" Nick asked taking a few steps toward her.

"I can take him back to the inn. I have to drive that way anyway to get back to Jackson," Audrey said.

"That's so kind of you, Audrey," Bella said, a little too politely, as if she was trying too hard.

"But Bella was going to teach me how to hurl a snowball and make a direct hit," Gavin said loud enough so Bella could hear him.

She turned to him. "Some other time, Gavin. I'm sorry."

Bella continued her rush to the front door, grabbed her coat and walked out with Travis trailing right behind her.

Chapter Seven

Bella was off the porch and high-tailing it to her truck so quickly that Travis could barely keep up with her.

"Bella, wait," he called but she kept right on walking, the snow crunching under her feet.

The woman was relentless once she made up her mind to do something. She left him no choice so he did the only thing he could think of to get her attention: he threw a wet snowball at her. It made contact with her sweet butt as he took pride in his aim.

"Yes!"

She jumped and turned around, staring as if she wasn't quite sure what to do next. This could go either way. He waited, breathing hard as snow began to fall.

"Do you even know how much you hurt me?" She yelled it as if she was well and truly riled, not to mention losing control.

"It was a snowball, not a rock," he yelled back as he moved toward her. "But I'm sorry if it hurt."

She didn't move. He could see raw emotion brewing on her face and wondered what the heck was upsetting her to the brink of tears. He felt helpless, as if she had built up a fortress around her and nothing and no one could ever break through.

"You don't get it, do you?" she asked him.

"I know it's not the smack on the butt with a snowball, but other than that, no. I don't get why you're so upset. Maybe if you gave me a clue."

"You can't be that naive."

He now stood right in front of her and could see the emotion burning on her face. Again he reached out for her, and again she pulled away.

"Come on, Bella. I'm a guy. It comes with the DNA."

"You're a Granger."

"Yeah, and…?"

"Didn't you learn anything from your dad?"

"Apparently nothing that can help me out with understanding you."

"You're impossible!"

"Me? I'm a straight shooter. No misfires with this ole cowboy. Everything is out in the open. Nothing hidden in my barn but hay."

He caught the smirk she tried to suppress. "And you expect me to believe you after all the games you've been playing since I arrived?"

"Games? Me? You've got me mistaken with some other cowboy."

"I know that you and your family, along with my conniving dad, are all trying to get me to back down, to return to Chicago and leave my dad right here in Briggs running that money pit."

"Nobody wants you to leave Briggs, Bella, especially not me."

"That's never going to happen."

He rested his hands on her arms. He could feel her tremble through her coat. "Your dad's given up. I won't."

"You gave up on me a long time ago."

His voice got low. "I never gave up on you, Bella."

"You broke my heart."

"If I did, that was never my intention."

"You should have written back to me. Answered my letters. Sent me an email. Found me on a search engine."

Her eyes watered.

"You're ripping your dad from his home because you're angry at me over my social-media skills? This may come as a surprise to you, but I have better things to do with my time than sit in front of a computer all day."

Anger flared on her face. "Don't flatter yourself."

She moved away from his grasp and immediately headed for her truck and got in. Just as she turned over the engine, Travis jumped into the passenger seat barely getting the door closed before she backed up and drove up the road.

Looking at her, and seeing how she was navigating the slippery road, he was glad his footing had been steady.

"Bella, you need to tell me what's going on. You could always talk to me when we were kids. That was the one thing we both had, no matter what."

"What's going on between my dad and Audrey? He never mentioned her during any of his calls or emails."

This was not the question Travis had expected, but he tried to answer it as best he could. "He doesn't say much about her, but I think she's his good friend."

"They're a lot more than friends."

After tonight, Travis knew that was true, but he didn't know the facts so he wasn't about to spread assumptions.

"I never asked and Nick never told me anything other than the friend part. It's none of my business."

"Does she live in Briggs?"

"No. In Jackson."

She quickly gazed at Travis, and he caught the concern on her face. "How long have they been dating?"

"I don't know."

"Were they dating when he was married to my mom?"

His breath hitched as he turned to face her. "Whatever gave you that idea?"

"My dad spent a lot of time in Jackson when I was a kid."

She momentarily drove off the road until she turned the wheel into the skid and got them back on course. Travis didn't move or say a word as they were sliding, hoping like heck she knew how to right the situation. When she did, he was hugely grateful.

"That doesn't mean he was cheating on your mom."

"Maybe not, but it would explain a lot."

"You're jumping the fence without the horse."

"What the heck does that mean?"

He turned to face her. Her features looked tight, and her chin was extended, a sure sign she was getting angry. He needed to calm her down, especially seeing as how she was driving…in the snow.

"It means your dad is a good man and I'd trust him with my life. A man like that would never cheat on anything or anyone, let alone on your mom. I'm sure this friendship he has with Audrey is something that happened long after your parents divorced."

She didn't say anything for a few minutes, and instead took a few deep breaths and let them out slowly, as if she'd practiced the method several times before.

Finally, as she drove out onto the main road that lead back to town she began talking.

"I work for an amazing company. I make more money than I ever thought possible. My apartment overlooks the lake and I have friends who are upwardly mobile like I am. Briggs is a small town that my mom was right to leave and although she left for some crazy reasons, she did what she thought she needed to do. In the long run, it was probably for the best."

"Do you really believe that?"

"Yes," she whispered.

Travis didn't believe her.

"Then why did you get so emotional when my family brought up our little Christmas tree?"

"Because you never once wrote and told me that story. I would've loved to know that your family celebrated Christmas in front of our tree. Heck, I would've loved to know just about anything to do with you or your family. I missed you all so much."

"I did write. Several times, but each time my letters were returned, unopened."

"We moved a lot. Still, you should have kept trying."

"I was thirteen years old. My attention span was about as good as a colt, always darting to the next adventure. I'm truly sorry."

"Jaycee wrote and told me as soon as I left you started hanging out with the popular girls at school. My heart broke. You always said you didn't like them, that you'd rather be with me, yet you turned right around and took up with them as soon as I left."

"I was forced to do a project with two of them. Jaycee had it all wrong. She should have never told you that."

"The other night at the bar, there you were with the same girls. Are you dating one of them?"

"I'm not dating anyone. Are you?"

"No."

"Why?"

"I don't have the time. What about you?"

"Just haven't found the right girl."

"According to my dad, my mother took me away because she was afraid I'd get pregnant with your baby and never accomplish anything with my life."

"We were kids. It would never have gone that far."

"Maybe not, but apparently she thought she was breaking some sort of cycle by leaving my dad and moving us to Chicago. I was born when my mom was only seventeen. Her own mother, my grandma, was pregnant at fifteen and married my grandpa to cover it up. That baby only lived for a few days. It had something wrong with its lungs. My gram didn't get pregnant again until way later in her life. That's when my mom was born."

"So your mom left Briggs to protect you?"

"I guess so, but it still hurts that my dad didn't fight harder for me."

"Plus, I seemingly gave up on you."

She nodded as tears rolled down her cheeks.

"I'm so sorry. I never gave up on you. Never. I should have worked harder at contacting you."

"Yes, you should have."

"I know that now, and I am sorry."

"Thank you."

"Would it help if I told you that it was hell not seeing you every day, especially after my mom passed? I needed you more than ever. I could talk to my dad and my brothers about it, but none of them were you. Your dad was the closest thing I had to you, so I gravitated to him hoping he'd call you while I was visiting and I'd get to talk to you. But he never called and after a while, I stopped hoping."

It was the first time Travis had admitted that to anyone. He didn't know how much more he should tell her. Still, he couldn't stop himself. "Once my mom passed I never could understand why you weren't closer to your dad. Sure he didn't follow you and your mom to Chicago, but he was alive and living right here in Briggs. You could've seen him anytime you wanted to. Why didn't you ever fly out for Christmas or for the summer? I never got that."

"Because my mom wouldn't let me." The words came tumbling out as if a dam had broken and the flood of emotion couldn't be held back any longer.

Tears fell freely down her cheeks.

She sucked in a deep breath and he watched as she tried to wipe the tears away with her fingers. Everything in him wanted to cradle her in his arms and tell her he was there for her, but reason told him she wouldn't accept his embrace…at least not yet.

"Bella, I'm sorry you lost your mom last year. Losing a parent is never easy."

"Thanks. Even though I'm mad at her right now for taking me away, I miss her like crazy. She was the one person I could always turn to for advice. I miss her hugs the most. She had a way of wrapping me in her arms so I felt safe and protected. My mom was a strong woman. Maybe a little too strong at times. She kept me away from my dad for no good reason, and I don't know if I can ever forgive her for that… Divorce sucks."

"Losing a parent, no matter what the reason, sucks."

She pulled the truck up in front of Dream Weaver Inn, turned off the ignition, hesitated before she told him goodnight and left him sitting there. Emotion overtook him as he watched the love of his life walk into the inn and close the door behind her.

He knew there was no hope for any kind of reconciliation at this point. If she hadn't turned to him now, she probably never would. As much as it tore his heart apart, he knew it was time to let her go.

BELLA SPENT MOST of the night coming to terms with everything she'd learned about her dad and his girlfriend, about her mom and about Travis. Now, as sunshine poured in through the windows in her room, all Bella wanted to do was heal from the emotional roller coaster she'd been on ever since she'd arrived in Briggs.

Bella couldn't think of anything other than what a dope she'd been all these years. She felt as though she'd been living in an acceptance bubble and had never tried to step outside of it. Why she hadn't questioned anything her mom told her was beyond comprehension, and now that she was gone, Bella would never get to tell her just how much pulling her away from Briggs because of her mom's own fears had really hurt.

She showered, dressed and hurried down to the kitchen to grab a quick breakfast. The inn was eerily quiet and gave her a chill as she walked along the deserted hallway knowing that every room was now vacant. Even when she was a little girl and times got rough, the inn was never completely empty. There were always at least one or two rooms occupied. The knowledge that she and her dad were possibly the only two people in the building sent a jolt of fear through her.

Fear that the final sale could actually be real. That the inn would finally belong to someone else and that someone else wouldn't be a person, but a corporation.

That realization wasn't sitting well with her on this fine Briggs morning, especially when she caught sight of a good portion of the town folk out the side window carving snow in the empty lot next door. It had snowed again last night, at least another three or four inches, which seemed to add to the event going on right outside the kitchen window.

Bella immediately spotted Amanda with her pink hair and her loving husband, Milo, close by, along with most of the Granger clan, including Travis. Dusty Spenser and his wife were out there along with almost everyone else she'd seen at Belly Up. They all seemed to be having a good time carving everything from teddy bears to entire towns out of huge squares of snow, some of them taller than the carvers.

Everyone thoroughly enjoying the magical moments of Christmas.

Everyone except Bella.

As she watched half the town out there in the snow, while she stood inside, alone in the kitchen, she allowed herself to feel the longing once again for her hometown. She concentrated on her emotions, on her nostalgia while the coffeepot gurgled out its remaining liquid, while she scrambled two eggs, buttered a piece of toast then sat on the chair next to the table to eat what she'd prepared. And she realized how much she longed to be outside with everyone else, to be part of the snow-sculpting contest, to be part of her hometown, Briggs, Idaho.

Maybe it wasn't too late....

"All signed on the dotted line." Her father's voice echoed through the kitchen as he dropped the stack of papers on the table in front of Bella. She hadn't heard him come in and his voice had startled her.

He came around the table and leaned on the counter in front of her as she found composure and reason.

"What do you mean? When did you sign these?"

She fanned through the pages and sure enough, there was his familiar illegible signature scrawled on every page on the highlighted lines.

"The first night you arrived."

She gazed up at him, unable to grasp what he'd said. Her dad was dressed in a navy wool coat. A black knit hat concealed his hair, creased jeans covered his long legs and brown snow boots were on his feet. His nose was still pink from the cold.

"What? These have been signed the whole time?"

"Of course they have. I just thought you might change your mind if you hung around awhile and saw what you were missing. I took a chance, but I can see now, that was a pointless idea."

Looking back, Bella wished he'd given them to her right away. She'd rather have kept her emotions hidden and flown back to Chicago in a blissful real-estate high than be second-guessing herself like she'd been all morning.

"Why didn't you give them to me that first night? We could be sitting pretty right now on a sandy beach."

"In Orlando?"

"Tampa."

"Whatever." He sat in the chair across from her at the table. "Honey, this is the most time I've spent with you in fifteen years. If I'd given them to you that first night, I'd be living on my own by now in some retirement home, trying to build up excitement about a round of golf."

"We've barely seen each other."

"But you were here, sleeping at the inn again, asking me for cinnamon milk, sharing a dinner at the Grangers' and skating with Travis at Skaits. All the things you liked when you were a kid. Maybe now we can have a relationship, now that you know I'd do anything for you. I only hope you'll have more time for me while I'm living in Orlando."

She knew he was pulling her chain. "Dad."

"Okay. Okay. Tampa. I don't know the first thing about that part of Florida, but I'll give it a whirl if it means you and I can have some fun together. Maybe play a little golf?"

"I'd like that." She slid off her stool and hugged him, a real honest-to-goodness hug this time. "You'll see. You'll like it there. The condo I bought for you is fabulous. It's on the seventh tee. You can see almost the entire course from your back patio."

"Sounds great, really great."

They pulled apart. "Did I detect some sarcasm there?"

"Me. No. Never. But what about Travis?"

"What about him?" Bella needed to dispel any hope her dad had that the two of them would somehow get together again.

"You and him gonna be friends or what? That man loves you. Always has, and probably always will."

"We're friends, but that's it. I've changed so much since we were kids. If he is in love with me, which I doubt, he's in love with the idea of me, not the real me."

Nick smiled and shook his head. "I know that boy

like he was my own son and you got him all wrong. Give him a chance. You might be surprised."

She pulled away from her dad and sat back down on her stool, took a sip of her coffee and thought about what it would mean to have Travis Granger really in love with her.

"It would never work, Dad. I can't live here, and he can't live anywhere else but on the Granger ranch."

"That may be true, sweetheart, but I know what I see. Two people who were meant to be together."

"Exactly what I saw between you and Audrey. Why didn't you tell me about her?"

"She's none of your concern."

"Are you shutting me out?"

He stared at the floor for a moment, then back at Bella. "She's a good friend, is all."

"And you're fine with leaving this so called 'friend' to move across the country."

"If that's what it takes for me to finally have a relationship with you, then yes. I'm ready to go."

"Dad, don't—"

"I've made up my mind. I lost you once. I'm not losing you again. Never mind about me. What about you and Travis? You really going to leave him again?"

Bella took a bite of her now cold eggs. "There's nothing there to leave. All that romance stuff is fine for novels and movies but it's not reality. We're too different now."

He shrugged. "That's not how I see it."

Bella didn't want to talk about Travis anymore. "Shouldn't you be out there carving a city or something?"

"I already finished. Travis told me what happened

last night on the way home from dinner with the Grangers and I figured we were done trying to convince you to stay."

"Is that what all this was about? You guys wanted me to stay?"

"Of course we did, sugar. Still do. He and I've been wanting you to stay ever since you arrived."

TRAVIS HADN'T SEEN Bella all day. He'd been too busy running the snow-sculpting contest to call on her, and apparently she hadn't cared enough to come looking for him, even though he was right outside her door. He thought he'd spotted her a couple times through the kitchen window watching some of the contestants while they worked, but she never made her presence known.

The contest had been a total success, with Amanda and Milo taking first prize with their rendition of Dream Weaver Inn. Travis thought the town gave it the blue ribbon for nostalgic reasons rather than for its detail and beauty. That win went to Phyllis Gabaur and her two grandkids who carved a miniature cowboy up on his horse. Phyllis tried to steal the blue ribbon, like she always did whenever she didn't win it for whatever contest she entered, but this time her grandkids stopped her thieving ways.

In the end, everyone seemed happy and the sculptures would remain on display, illuminated by spotlights courtesy of the local fire department's generators, until mid-January.

It had been a long day, and the night had only just begun. Travis contemplated grabbing a fast dinner in town when he spotted Bella standing in the town square. She watched as a line of children waited to talk to Santa-Milo. He sat in a giant red chair in the middle of a white gazebo strung with white lights as three elves, teens from the local high school, handed out homemade candy canes from the ladies of the Red Hat Society after each child sat on Santa's lap. With the backdrop of all the twinkling lights on the row of pine trees that encircled the park, the lights and ornaments on the main tree, and all the people milling around her, Bella looked about as pretty as he'd ever seen her. She wore a white fuzzy knit hat, scarf and matching gloves. Her black coat was buttoned up tight, her jeans hugged her legs and her new calf-high gray boots, suitable for snow, made her appear taller than her actual height. He longed to walk right up to her, take her in his arms and kiss her. But he restrained himself and instead, smiled his welcome as he approached her knowing full well that any chance he had with her was over. Nick told him he'd signed the paperwork and given it to Bella that morning.

The defeat had saddened Travis more than he thought possible, but from the look on Nick's face when he'd told Travis, it had torn him up even more.

Now, as Travis approached her and she turned toward him, a friendly smile creased her lips...probably due to her win with her dad. It occurred to Travis how different her reaction was compared to his and Nick's and it reinstated what he already knew.

Bella Biondi had grown up city and wanted no part of country.

Amen to that.

"Is that Milo Gump playing Santa in the Gazebo?"

"Sure is."

"It's the perfect role for him. The town looks magical."

"I don't think I heard you right. Did you say the town looks magical?"

She nodded. "Yes. It's lovely."

He stared at her. "Just when I think I have you figured out, you say something like that."

"What? Am I wrong?"

"No. Not at all. You finally said something…" But he stopped himself, not wanting to say what he was thinking. "I was going to grab a bite to eat. Want to join me?"

"Love to, thanks."

They started walking across the street together as Travis contemplated this new situation with a Bella who seemed more like the laid-back girl he'd known rather than the obstinate woman he'd only recently met.

"Come to think of it, there are some really nice tasting booths in the square serving hot food. That might be more fun than sitting down to a regular meal. Are you up for it?"

"I'm up for anything."

And with those words, Travis decided this must be how Bella reacted to getting her way. He wasn't sure he liked the fact that she'd be leaving soon to close the deal on her father's inn, but he sure liked the change in her personality as a result.

He decided to go with it and enjoy these final moments with her.

For the next hour, he and Bella tried various specialties from the different restaurants that were represented at the booths: fried calamari from Gino's Fishy Fridays, sweet and sour pork from Wok n' Roll, thick cut crispy fries from The Spud House, and a generous slice of Sweet Potato pie from The Pie Hole. They washed it all down with hot apple cider from Apple Ever After, a fresh-juice bar.

As they were finishing up Dodge and Edith strolled by and Bella made a point of apologizing to them. "I'm sorry I left so abruptly last night, but I—"

"No need to apologize for anythin'. You got a perfect right to do whatever it is you got a mind to do," Dodge said as he gave her a tight hug.

Edith also gave her a hug. "It's a beautiful night, now you two run along and have some fun." She turned to Travis. "Isn't it about time you pulled out that sleigh of yours?"

"I'd love to go for a ride," Bella said.

Travis had planned on getting it out later that night, after he'd dropped off Bella, but looking at her smiling face, he couldn't believe her response.

"Wait. Did you just say you'd like to go for a ride?"

Her face beamed. "Yep, seems like the perfect night for it."

The sky sparkled with a million stars as a half-moon hung like a beacon over the Teton mountain range.

"Anything for you, darlin'."

And they took off for the inn.

WHILE TRAVIS READIED the sleigh and horses, Bella went up to the main house. She wanted to slip on another sweater under her coat. She expected to see the inn in darkness, but instead it was ablaze with lights. Even the hokey life-size Santa and reindeer on the roof were lit and there was music and voices coming from the lobby.

A twinge of anger coursed through her veins as she approached the front door and saw a roomful of people gathered inside around her dad's baby grand piano, but it quickly dissipated when she reminded herself she had the signed paperwork for the sale in her briefcase.

Truth be told, she wasn't sure if the fact that the deal was going through made her happy or sad. If seeing her dad playing his piano again brought out more pain and heartache or made her happy.

All those years, lost. All those Christmases spent trying to ignore the holiday when Chicago's Michigan Avenue turned into a virtual winter wonderland at Christmas. All that time she could have spent with her dad...stripped away from her by an overprotective mom.

She pushed open the front door and immediately her senses were overloaded with childhood smells and sounds she'd long since forgotten. Cinnamon and pine permeated the air. The fireplace gave off the sweet scent of burning wood. The lights were dimmed and the tree sparkled. There had to be at least fifty people in the tiny room, all singing her favorite Christmas carol, "It's Beginning to Look a Lot Like Christmas."

Her eyes instantly misted over as she listened to the room filled with neighbors belting out the tune. She thought of all the times she and her dad had sat side by side at that piano singing that very song. They were good memories and now she added one more to the list...the last memory.

Audrey sat next to him on the piano bench, playing her part on the keys. They sang out the chorus, smiling at each other as if they knew each other's nuances, as if they'd been intimate with each other. Up until last night, Bella never considered that her dad might be dating someone. Why hadn't he told her? That would've changed everything. She had always pictured him a lonely older man, pining over his lost wife and child. Not a guy courting a woman from the next town.

A male voice somewhere behind her distracted her attention from her dad and the dark-haired beauty on the bench. "Too bad Nick's daughter sold this inn right out from under him."

A woman's voice said, "I hear she's a real Scrooge."

Another man's voice said, "How does someone kick out the guests and fire the entire staff just days before Christmas?"

"Someone who has no heart, that's who," the woman said.

"This town won't be the same without Nick, and Nick won't be the same without this town," the first man added.

"I wish she'd never come home. She certainly doesn't belong here anymore," the woman remarked.

"That's for sure," yet another male voice said.

If Bella could snap her fingers and fly out of Briggs at that precise second, she would have. Everyone hated her, and with good reason. As she looked around at the smiling faces, and watched as her dad entertained everyone, for the first time since she left Briggs with her mom, she realized why her dad couldn't have gone with them. Why he had insisted on staying and running the inn. Why he'd been pretending to drag his feet about signing the paperwork. Her dad was in love with the town, and when a man was in love, nothing else mattered.

"Ready?" Travis asked as he tapped her on the shoulder.

She turned and at first glance she didn't recognize

him. His beard was pure white and he wore a bright red cowboy hat.

"What's all this?" she asked tugging on his whiskers.

"I'll tell you in the sleigh. We're running late."

Then as if it was as natural as snowflakes, he took her hand and led her out the door, but before he'd turned she caught the look on his face, the same look her dad had while he was singing: the look of pure joy.

Chapter Eight

"Where are we going?" Bella asked once she was tucked in under the blanket. This time she liked the sensation of touching his leg with hers, of being close to him under a sky now heavy with snow clouds. "And what's under the tarp in the back?"

The entire back of the sleigh was covered with a deep red tarp. If Bella didn't know better she'd think she was going for a ride in Santa's sleigh.

"A surprise for a lot of important people."

"Don't tell me you're Santa."

"Milo Gump is the town's Santa. I'm just a cowboy—"

"With a white beard."

"How do you like it?" He mugged for her.

"Cute."

"You're cute. I'm supposed to look manly."

"…in a Santa sort of way."

He hesitated and she thought he was going to kiss her again, but instead he said, "Ready?"

"Yep. Let's get this rig moving."

And with that he snapped the reigns and the regal Clydesdales took off as if they already knew their destination. He took a route that avoided the cleared roads and instead stayed on back roads which were still caked with snow and ice. They glided over the roads giving Bella the feeling they were floating. The horses' hooves made a distinctive clomping sound as they pulled the sleigh. Bella couldn't stop smiling as she threaded her arm through Travis's and held on tight.

Fifteen minutes later he pulled up in front of the Teton Valley Hospital, jumped down and secured his horses to a special Santa post as several of the medical staff, both men and women, all wearing Santa hats, came rushing out to greet him. Bella carefully stepped down out of the sleigh, trying to act as excited as everyone else, but she had no idea what they were doing at the hospital. Travis peeled off his coat to reveal a bright red flannel shirt over his black jeans and black cowboy boots. Then he grabbed a great big red sack which someone had pulled out from under the tarp and slung it over his shoulder. Moments later he walked toward the glass doors while three of the staff members lugged in smaller red fuzzy sacks right behind him.

One of the staff members, a girl in her early twenties wearing blue scrubs handed Bella a smaller sack and a red cowgirl hat. "Cowboy Santa needs all the help he can get," the girl said. Then she giggled and followed the group inside.

The concept that Travis Granger was known as Cowboy Santa and apparently handed out presents at the local hospital was almost too much for Bella to take in. Did the man have no vices? Was he always this generous? Was he some kind of saint? Compared to her, he was all those things and more. The townsfolk at the inn who were badmouthing her were right. Not only didn't she belong in the town, she most certainly didn't belong with Travis Granger: Cowboy Santa.

Bella had a choice to make. She could call a cab, go back to the inn, pack and catch the next plane out of the Teton Valley or she could help Travis and his helpers deliver the presents.

She reached for her phone to call the cab when she caught sight of Travis on the other side of the glass double doors and waved at her to follow him inside. Without hesitation she slid her phone back in her pocket, secured the red cowgirl hat on her head, flung the sack over her shoulder and took off for the double glass doors.

"Wait for me!" she called and ran to catch up.

For the next few hours the group handed out presents to some of the most grateful people Bella had ever met. Each patient seemed both surprised and thankful. Everyone, that is, except for Harry B. Truman, an eighty-something man who cussed and yelled when Bella and Travis entered his room bearing gifts.

"Get out! Get out!"

Then he flung his plastic cup in their direction and yelled some of the foulest language Bella had ever heard.

Bella and Travis high-tailed it out of there, but before they left, Bella noticed the picture of a shaggy-haired dog on the nightstand next to his bed. The dog wore two pink bows in its hair with the cutest little face Bella had ever seen. A man who kept a picture of a dog like that next to his hospital bed couldn't be all bad.

According to one of the nurses who helped deliver the gifts, a willowy girl in her early thirties named Lexi, Harry's problems began when a man in a Santa costume broke into his house several years ago and stole Harry's collection of snow globes. Harry had tried to stop the snow-globe thief, but the thieving Santa socked him in the jaw while his elves held him down. The bad Santa then stuffed all of Harry's snow globes in a sack and took off up the chimney.

"At least that was the story he gave to the local sheriff, and ever since then, whenever Harry sees a Santa, any kind of Santa, he has a panic attack and winds up here. Harry doesn't have any family in the valley so we take care of him during the holidays."

"What about his cute little dog?"

"I take care of Puddles when Harry's stuck in here. She's a sweetheart. Sometimes I sneak her in so Harry can visit with her. Don't tell anybody. I could lose my job."

"I promise," Bella said knowing perfectly well there was no one for her to tell.

As Travis and the group hustled away from Harry's room, Bella crept back in and gave Harry a soft-pink scarf despite the fact he told her he "didn't need no stinking gifts" and just wanted to be left alone. And he especially "didn't need no pink scarf."

But she left it, anyway.

A couple doors down an older lady with snow-white hair thanked Bella several times for her new knit hat, which she promptly slipped on her head. "If you keep your head warm, your whole body stays warm," she told Bella as she pulled the hat down over her ears.

In another room, Bella met a man who looked like he might be in his eighties, sitting in a wheelchair. He blessed her for giving him a new pair of slippers.

An attractive middle-aged woman gave Bella an unopened box of candy in exchange for the lovely French soap Bella insisted she take.

Every room she and Travis visited caused Bella to

tear up when she left. They all seemed to know Travis or know his family and if they didn't know the Grangers they knew her dad.

"Nick and I used to go fishing together when we were kids to get away from our parents in the summertime," a man around her dad's age told her. His name was Jimmy Prince and apparently he'd been a good friend. He seemed familiar to Bella, but she couldn't quite place him. "We'd sneak off in the afternoons and wouldn't get home until after dark. His mom would get so mad she'd threaten to whoop us both until she saw the load of fish we'd caught in the river. You tell your dad I'll be out to see him as soon as I get out of this dang place. They're making me stay when there's no need."

"I will," Bella told him, knowing her dad would be in Florida by the time Jimmy Prince got around to the visit. Jimmy was recovering from a broken hip.

Then in room three-forty-seven, a private room in the children's section, Bella met a little boy who warmed up to her like he'd been part of her life since he was born.

"What's your name, little man?" Bella asked, his cherub face beaming at the sight of Travis. In turn, Travis seemed to enjoy kids more than Bella thought a single guy could. And not just his nieces and nephews, but all kids. He knew exactly how to get a child to relax or giggle and he always spoke to them with respect, a trait Bella was learning.

In the past, she barely spoke to children, let alone had a respectful conversation with anyone under the age of puberty, and even then it was doubtful the conversation would amount to anything but awkward small talk. She'd ask a question and they'd give her a yes or no response. Not much communication going on there.

"Georgie." His voice was barely audible. The sweet little boy with the curly dark hair and big sad eyes looked up at Travis. "Are you Cowboy Santa? My mom promised me you'd stop by tonight and here you are. My mom never lies."

"Yep, and this here is my helper, Cowgirl Santa."

Georgie held out his hand for Bella to shake. She took it and immediately felt that his body temperature was too warm.

Georgie giggled. "I never met Cowgirl Santa before." He tried to push himself up in his big bed, but couldn't quite do it. Travis pressed a button and the back of his bed lifted.

"Then this is a first." Bella raked his mop of curly hair off his forehead and noticed he was sweating. Apprehension surged through her as she wondered what was wrong with Georgie to make him sweaty and in a hospital bed so close to Christmas.

"Did you bring me a pony?" Georgie asked as he strained to look behind Travis.

"You know they won't let ponies in a hospital," Travis told him. "That would be against all the rules and you know how strict hospitals are about their rules."

Crestfallen, Georgie protested. "I know, but it's the only thing I ever wanted. I asked for a pony last year, too, but Santa didn't bring it. I thought for sure you would bring me a pony."

"Now why's that? If Santa can't do it, what makes you think I can?"

"'Cause you're a cowboy and cowboys ride horses. Everybody knows that."

"Tell you what, as soon as you get out of here I'll

take you for a ride in my sleigh. You can hold on to the reins. How's that?"

That didn't appease Georgie, and big tears slid down his cheeks. "Okay," he said, rubbing the tears away with his little fists.

It broke Bella's heart.

She was about to offer to buy the child a pony when a familiar voice echoed behind her.

"Georgie, sweetheart, Cowboy Santa can't bring you a pony. It wouldn't fit in his sleigh."

"Oh, Mama, I want one so bad."

Bella turned to see her friend Jaycee step up to the bed and soothe her little boy. She gave him a hug, rubbed his back and offered him the juice box on the tray next to his bed.

Georgie didn't take the juice, but he did stop crying.

"Somehow, I knew you'd be here tonight," Jaycee said as she hugged Bella so tight she had a difficult time breathing. "You're such a sweetheart."

"Thanks." The word stuck in Bella's throat as emotion and concern for Georgie welled up inside her.

"He's doing really well this time, and we should be able to take him home by Christmas Eve," Jaycee said as if Bella already knew why Georgie was in the hospital.

But she didn't and no one seemed to be offering the information. Whatever it was that had brought Georgie to the hospital seemed to be something serious and it broke Bella's heart to know that such a courageous boy was so sick.

The entire evening had proven to be unsettling to Bella, and rewarding at the same time, especially after she peeked into Harry's room and saw that he'd wrapped the scarf around his neck. Never in her adult life had she felt such a mix of emotions in one night and it was all due to Cowboy Santa. He truly was a special man, but then she'd always known that since they were kids. He would give away almost anything he owned if he thought someone needed it more than he did. Plus, he would do almost anything for a friend, and especially for a girlfriend. She'd sometimes make him wear her grandpa's clothes and hat, and not once did he ever complain, even when she'd make him walk into town and the other kids made fun of him. He'd just smile and tip his big hat.

Travis Granger had stolen her heart a long time ago and no other man would ever have the key.

"Where are we going next?" Bella asked once she and Travis were back in the sleigh. It had turned into a windy, cold night, with cornflake-sized snow falling from the heavens. Bella slipped on the silly puppet gloves, the only gloves she could find in her purse. She took his arm and pressed in closer then she opened her mouth, tilted her head up to the sky, stuck out her tongue and waited for a snowflake to land. She felt like a kid, like a happy, dizzy kid amazed by the magic of snow.

When snowflakes not only landed on her tongue but on her eyes and nose and cheeks, goose bumps danced over her entire body.

She closed her mouth, looked over at Travis and giggled.

"Thank you for that."

"For what?"

"For letting me watch you act like a kid again."

"You can watch me anytime."

"Is that a promise?"

She chuckled. "What do you have in mind?"

He smirked and lifted an eyebrow. "My place is less than a mile from here and it might be easier if we spent the night there…in separate bedrooms, of course."

"Of course," she said as she tipped her head back to the sky and moved in closer, giggling every time a snowflake touched her face.

ONCE TRAVIS SECURED the team in the heated corral behind his house, he and Bella hurried inside. At least four inches of snow had collected on the ground and the drifts were almost as tall as Bella. Getting back to his house had been a challenge, but with Bella by his side keeping him warm, and his strong Clydesdale team leading the way, Travis knew they'd all get home safe.

"I think we just made it before those roads became impassable," Travis said as he unlocked the back door to the mud room, and flicked on the lights. Bella sat on the bench he'd made that last summer, and removed her boots, then hung her coat and scarf on one of the hooks above her. Travis did the same. She took off her gloves and shoved them in the back pocket of her jeans. His hat went up on the shelf along with hers and his many other hats. He estimated he owned somewhere between fifteen and twenty Western hats, a fact his dad always made fun of. His dad owned three, one for the summer, one for the winter and one for dress up. According to Dodge, "a cowboy don't need more than three hats, any more than that and he's a milliner not a cowboy."

Travis opened the kitchen door and hit the switch for the lights. As soon as Bella stepped inside a great big smile spread across her face and her eyes lit up like they used to when they were younger. He wanted to pick her up and take her directly to his bedroom and make love to her. Her naked body lying under his was about all he could think of on the ride home, how her skin would feel when he touched her, how she would taste, how he would kiss her lips, her neck, her breasts, her belly, her...

"Oh, Travis, this place is charming."

She broke his trance, which was probably a good thing considering all the adrenaline that was pumping through his veins. He tried to focus on his house and giving her a tour.

"Would you like to see the rest of the place?" Each word was a struggle to get out, but by darn he would act like a gentleman even if it killed him.

"Yes, please," she said holding out her hand.

He took it and a spark shot out.

"Sorry about that," he said.

She giggled. "It tickled."

He encircled her soft hand, clearing his throat from the lump that was forming. He'd always dreamed that one day he'd show her his house, and now that it was happening emotion began to creep up inside him. Never in a million years would he have expected to feel such a rush of excitement as he guided her through the rooms he so carefully crafted and decorated. She stood next to him, and he realized he'd created this house and everything in it with Bella in mind. Funny how the unconscious mind took over even when he thought he was creating something entirely for his own comforts.

"I built this house almost exactly to the plans your dad and I drew up that winter you and your mom left. I added a second bathroom and a home office, but other than those two adjustments, we followed the plans, exactly."

The house had turned out to be the perfect respite for Travis. No matter what was going on in his life, once he stepped through the door, all his worries vanished like so much smoke.

He'd built the kitchen with glass front cabinetry, soapstone counter tops, a deep country sink, a six-burner industrial stove and installed a fridge with a glass door and a separate freezer hidden behind a cabinet door.

"The kitchen is perfect. I wouldn't change a thing," she said, letting go of his hand then walking through the large doorway into the dining room. She was like a kid in a toy store, eager to discover what wonders lay ahead. He stood back and watched as she seemed to marvel at it all. Travis had become an expert carpenter and craftsman, and each room contained his handiwork. Not only had he created his own crown molding and base boards, but he'd constructed his own mantels around the four fireplaces, one in the living room, the family room, the master bedroom and the loft.

"The house is beautiful, Travis, but I can't believe you didn't put up a tree."

"It's up in the loft," he told her, not wanting to go up there with her.

"There's a loft?"

"Yep. My nieces and nephews love it. It's more of a converted attic than anything else, but I opened up one side of it in the master bedroom."

She walked past him in the living room, and headed down the hall toward the bedrooms. He waited for her response and when he didn't hear her, he figured it was appropriate behavior for Scrooge Bella. She'd look at that room and think it was ridiculous, but part of him hoped the child in her might show up despite her adult dislike of all things Christmas.

He waited some more.

Nothing.

She didn't come out of the bedroom nor did he hear anything.

After a good ten minutes he thought he better make sure she hadn't fallen down the stairs or had some other type of accident.

When he entered the bedroom and walked around to the stairway, he called out her name, but didn't get a response. Panic tightened his chest and he took the stairs two at a time.

"Bella! Are you all right?"

Still no answer.

His heart beat heavy against his chest until he saw her, sitting cross-legged on the floor in front of the ceiling-high tree, wearing her tiara and her gram's black lace scarf, the trunk lid open in the corner of the decorated room. Travis had turned the loft into a Christmas room primarily for his nieces and nephews whenever they stopped by. He knew it made them happy. He hoped it had the same effect on Bella.

"How did you get all this? I saw those moving guys cart everything away."

Travis sat down on the floor next to her. "I couldn't let your trunk go. Not yet. I thought you might have a change of heart."

She nodded, and the tiara slipped sideways on her head making her look a little drunk. "You never gave up hope, did you?"

"About us? No, not really."

More tears flowed down her cheeks as she leaned in and kissed him, a salty kiss with all the passion Travis had wished for.

THEY KISSED BESIDE the tree for as long as they could tolerate the hard wooden floor, then Travis picked her up in his arms and carried her downstairs to his king-size bed. They fell onto the bed in a frenzy of arms and hands trying to pull off each other's clothes all the while kissing each other with such intensity that Bella felt she would faint from the excitement of it. Never in her life had she been kissed like that, and never had she felt such desire for any man as she felt for Travis.

She tugged on his whiskers. "I feel as if I'm making love with a naughty cowboy."

"If that's what it takes to turn you on, I'll never shave again."

She giggled and he kissed her again. Harder this time, with more urgency, his beard tickling her face and adding to her excitement.

When they were completely naked and his hands caressed her body she knew this was right, was always meant to be. His body felt hard and wonderful pressed up against hers and when he caressed her breasts and gently tugged on her nipples a fire bolted through her, causing her to moan with pleasure.

"I've been waiting a long time for this, Bella," he whispered in her ear, his breath hot, his voice raspy. A voice she'd never heard before.

"Me, too," she answered as she nibbled on his earlobe and caught her fingers in his thick hair.

She was on fire with desire for him, and wanted him to take her now. He pulled back and stared down at her body, the Christmas-tree lights from the loft throwing a warm golden glow on every surface it touched.

"You're more beautiful than I imagined," he told her with a smile on his lips.

He caressed her for a minute more, then leaned in and gently kissed her closed eyes, then her mouth, but stopped when she tried to bring him in tight on top of her.

"It's going to take me a little time to capture every part of you. I don't want to miss anything."

He moved back again gently stroking her body with his fingertips, lightly kissing her breasts, her nipples, her stomach, then going back to watching her move every time his fingers ran across her body. She tingled with anticipation for him, and goose bumps danced along her skin as his fingers danced over every curve.

"Do you even know how this is making me crazy?" she asked.

"Uh-huh. It's supposed to. I've been dreaming about seeing you naked for days. Now that you're here, in my bed, I don't want to rush it."

She couldn't help but smile as she arched her back and offered herself up to him with complete abandon. His smooth rhythm and tender touches slowly caused her to call out his name. Soon after, as her body trembled with pleasure, she reached her climax.

"You're so beautiful, Bella. So lovely to watch. To feel. To taste."

His words only added to her fever and when she thought she couldn't handle another minute, that she was completely spent, he slipped on a condom and gently entered her, and the excitement began to build once again.

This time, despite her thinking she couldn't possibly experience another orgasm, her lust for him increased with his every movement and when they reached their climax together she thought for sure her body would combust from the heat that surged through her veins.

Instead, the climax was deeper than she'd ever experienced with any other man, and the feeling of euphoria that flowed between them was almost more than she could understand. It felt as if years of pent-up emotions had finally been allowed to break free. She didn't want the experience to end, and she especially didn't want to cry in his arms. She'd done enough crying in the last few days.

He held her tight against his body while the minutes passed. Neither of them spoke. She knew she couldn't or the waterworks would begin and now she didn't think she could control them. It felt as if all those lonely years she'd lived without him, without her friends, without the comfort of her small town had finally come to an end. She was too frightened to say it out loud, terrified that he'd start making plans for her to stay, to move into his house, to be his wife one day.

She couldn't possibly see how that could happen.

This was just sex.

Nothing more.

Wasn't it?

But as she found herself drifting off to sleep in his arms a thought came crashing in. A thought that gave her a shiver so profound he must have felt it because he pulled the blanket up over them.

She was falling in love with him. Only this time, there was no one there to force her to leave.

Chapter Nine

Travis awoke in a kind of blissful haze, reaching out for Bella but finding only a jumble of cold blankets and sheets. He thought she must be in the kitchen cooking up some wonderful egg creation, that is if she could cook. Just because Nick was a natural, didn't mean it came naturally to Bella.

He quickly showered, thought about trimming his beard, but then flashed on how it seemed to turn her on the previous night and instead left it alone. He usually didn't shave it off until after Christmas, but this year, if Bella hung around, he decided he may just leave it be for a spell.

He finished cleaning up, got dressed in a sweater, jeans and his favorite Christmas socks, and went out to the kitchen to find Bella, imagining that she'd be standing behind the stove, naked except for a Santa hat.

The likelihood of that vision being a reality was slim to none, but a guy could dream.

He called out her name a few times to no response, and when he walked into the kitchen she wasn't there. He looked outside in the corral, but didn't see her anywhere. Then he went back to the bedroom and looked for her clothes.

They were gone.

Travis didn't understand why she would leave without telling him after they'd spent such an amazing night together. The only conclusion he could draw was there must be something wrong with either Nick or something bad had happened at the inn.

He immediately hightailed it out of there, calling Nick several times as he sped up the slippery roads. The plows had been out early that morning and most of the roads were fairly clean, but the surrounding trees were still heavy with white powder, as were the Teton Mountains in the distance.

When he finally pulled up in front of the inn, parked his truck and took stock of his surroundings, he noticed a large moving van parked alongside the inn, with a ramp leading up to open doors. He could hardly believe his eyes when he realized the roof Santa was gone, along with the N-O-E-L sign on the front lawn.

His heart pounded against his chest. There had to be some mistake. She couldn't go through with the sale. Not now. Not after last night.

Travis pushed open the front door only to find the room almost empty and three burly guys making preparations to carry out the piano. All the decorations were gone, even the Christmas tree had been stripped of all the ornaments. The mantel was bare and the banister on the stairway had been stripped of the festive garland his sister-in-law Maggie had spent an hour getting just right. He could see into the dining room and the tables were gone, the chairs were stacked up and the entire place was being ripped apart. A sense of dread swept over him. He now knew what tornado victims felt like when they witnessed the aftermath of destruction to their homes, their town. A mixture of sadness and nausea was taking hold and he had to work hard not to let those feelings overpower his reason.

When he spotted two men working on moving the piano out of the lobby irrational instinct took over.

"Wait! There has to be some mistake. I'll sort this out in a minute. Only please don't move that piano."

He yelled out for Nick, but didn't get an answer, instead Bella walked out from the back with another burly guy at her side. When she looked up and saw Travis, her face instantly drained of all its color.

"Travis, I can explain."

"I told these guys to wait. This is some kind of mistake, right?"

He could see the hesitation on her face before she spoke. "Travis, I—"

His breath caught in his throat, as if all the air had been knocked clean out of his lungs.

"Please don't tell me you're going through with the sale. Not after all that's happened. Not after last night."

She blushed. "You have to understand. I don't have a choice. This is business. TransGlobal phoned me early this morning and I—"

He walked over to her and looked into her eyes, wanting to see if there was even a shred of the girl he'd made love to in his bed mere hours before.

But he saw nothing. No emotion. Only Bella Biondi, real-estate mogul from Chicago.

"There's always a choice, Bella. No matter what, there's always a choice."

She glanced at the guy standing next to her, and when she gazed back at Travis, he saw anger in her eyes.

"Sometimes we all have to grow up and face the

facts. In business there are no choices. Once the ink dries, reality sets in. This is reality, Travis. My father has agreed to sell the inn. The paperwork is signed and TransGlobal will take possession in fifteen days. There's absolutely nothing anyone can do about it. Even you."

He felt physical pain as he watched the three men roll the now covered piano, sans its legs, out on a dolly.

Not only did he feel as though all the lovemaking meant nothing, but he felt as though a big part of him would never be the same. The sensations reminded him of when his mom took her last breath and there was nothing he could do to revive her. No medicine or words that could convince her to stay one more day.

Now as he studied Bella's beautiful face, he felt the same loss. The same heartache and the powerlessness of the emotion overtook him.

"I guess you're right, there's nothing I can do about it. Have a good life, Bella."

Then he turned and walked out just as she called for him one last time.

BELLA HAD TRIED to tell Travis she didn't have a choice. She wanted to explain that TransGlobal would sue her and her dad if she didn't go through with the deal. That she had already faxed over her dad's signed documents. And besides, she stood to lose over a million dollars on the deal. She'd have to be silly to give up that kind of money.

She needed Travis to understand, to support her decision, but apparently he didn't want to hang around and let her explain. Instead he told her in no uncertain terms they were through. What had been passionately rekindled was now over.

Forever.

She had lived without him before and she could do it again. She'd never been dumped by a lover before. This was something new. Normally she was the one who did the dumping.

Of course, with Travis there were no rules. Nothing was hard and fast with him, nothing but his ranch, his family and his stubborn streak. Why couldn't he see how important this deal was to her? Was he that blind with his own desires that he couldn't look past them to see hers?

She told herself she didn't need that kind of guy in her life, even if he was the one and only guy she ever loved. Even if he did make love to her like no other man. And even if he was Cowboy Santa.

It was time she stood tall and took back control of the situation. She knew better than to allow her emotions to dictate her business decisions, and selling her dad's inn was strictly business. Nothing more. Nothing less.

She'd called a cab that morning to take her back to the inn while he slept in his big, manly bed, alone. The only thing she couldn't find at his house was those darn Santa puppet gloves, so she'd slipped her hands in her pockets, hoping her fingers didn't freeze on the drive into town. She told herself those silly gloves didn't matter, but for some reason she couldn't shake having to leave them behind and every time she thought about not having them, she'd mist up. A ridiculous reaction to possibly the corniest gloves she'd ever seen.

Once back at the inn, she'd packed up all her things that had been scattered about her room and shoved her now overstuffed bags into her rented truck. Her dad had apparently done the same because when she went looking for him all his personal things were gone. She had no idea where he'd got to, but she suspected wherever he was Audrey was there with him.

"Ms. Biondi, we're all set. Every room is empty. All you need to do is sign the yellow copy and we'll be moving on." The tall man waiting beside her seemed like a nice enough guy. Probably had a loving family somewhere in the valley. Maybe he had a couple kids, a dog named Rover and a pretty little wife who did everything for him. Oh, and a white picket fence, too.

He stood to make a sizable chunk of change on her father's things. Probably enough so he could put a down payment on a new house, or send his kids to private school for a year and buy that new flat-screen TV he'd seen at a discount store.

All she had to do was sign on the dotted line and both their lives would improve.

But she didn't.

"Ms. Biondi? We can't leave unless you sign right here."

He shoved the clipboard with the paperwork in front of her, pointing to the dotted line. She looked down at it, noticed where she had to sign and took the pen he held out to her.

"When will you hold the auction?" she asked, stalling for time.

"After the holidays. It's too difficult right now. Maybe sometime in mid-January after everything calms down and the kids are back in school."

"Do you have any kids?"

"Me? No." He shook his head. "Don't want any kids.

Too much of a liability. I'm more of the free-spirit kind of guy."

She held the pen over the paper, but still couldn't sign.

"What about your wife? Doesn't she want kids?"

"Not married. Footloose and fancy free, that's my motto."

She always thought she was a good judge of character. What did this mean for her past deals? Had she been wrong about all her clients? Or was this affliction something new? Something she'd gleaned in Briggs, like the flu or a bad cold.

"You stand to make a sizable sum of money from all of this furniture."

His features suddenly took on a harder look. "I gave you a fair market price. If I make a few bucks at auction then it's a good deal. Most of the time, I hardly break even."

She knew he was exaggerating. "You can't stay in business if you don't make a profit."

He shifted his feet, and inched the clipboard closer to her.

"Look, lady. I got another business to stop at this afternoon, but before I do, I gotta unload all your stuff and put it in my warehouse. Are you gonna sign or not 'cause I got better things to do than stand here and argue over the virtues of being married or my profit margin."

"And I've got a cleaning crew coming in less than fifteen minutes, so we have to come to terms."

"What do you want from me?"

It was times like these that got under Bella's skin. She didn't like being pushed and she most certainly didn't like giving up all her father's things to some guy who obviously prided himself on taking advantage of a situation.

"Please bring the piano back inside, and I'll sign."

No way would she give up her dad's piano, the most expensive item on the truck to this guy. Instead, she decided to ship it to her dad in Florida. It would serve as a piece of home for him, and maybe he'd make friends easier because of it.

"I already got it loaded. And if I bring it back, I'll have to pay you less."

"How much less?"

"A thousand."

"Four hundred."

He smirked. She stood her ground.

"Seven hundred," he offered.

"Five hundred, and not a dime less. You made out like a bandit on all this stuff. Unload the piano, and put it back…carefully, or I won't sign."

They stared at each other intently. She could tell Mr. Footloose was knocking around the pros and cons of the deal.

So she did what she thought was necessary to close the deal in her favor.

She walked out and left Mr. Fancy Free standing in the empty lobby, contemplating his next move while she went off to say goodbye to her best friend.

"What's wrong with Georgie?" Bella asked Jaycee. The two women sat across from each other in the hospital cafeteria drinking surprisingly good coffee and nibbling on a cookie the size of a tall man's shoe. Georgie was fast asleep up in his hospital room and Jaycee's husband was home tending to their other two children.

Bella had wanted a long visit with Georgie, but sleep had overcome him five minutes into their conversation.

"He's going to be fine. Nothing to worry about. His doctors say this is easy to control. I'm sure a woman like you has more important things on her mind than my son."

Bella reached out across the table and laid her hand on top of Jaycee's. "Nothing is more important than a sick child."

Jaycee's eyes watered as she took a ragged breath. "Georgie has asthma and every now and then he gets a bad attack. This last one landed him in the hospital. Georgie loves animals, but he's really allergic to the dander. It's so hard to keep him away. He knows he can't go near horses, but sometimes he can't help himself, and I don't always have the heart to stop him. He's so little and helpless. His doctor told me he'd be fine with minimum exposure, but apparently it was enough to keep him in here for a few days."

"I'm so sorry. It must be scary for you to see him suffer like this."

"He'll be better once we move. There's a sweet little bungalow in town that we heard might be up for sale in a few months. It's on Main Street, within walking distance to everything. We're hoping to put an offer on it as soon as it goes on the market. Fred and me have been saving to buy our own house for the past couple of years, one without an old stable behind it. That's why Georgie wants a horse. He thinks because we have a stable in back of the house we rent, there should be horses living inside of it. He doesn't understand that those horses would make him sick."

Jaycee took a sip of her coffee, gazed around at the

people milling about, smiled at a nurse, nodded toward another then looked back at Bella. She seemed so composed, so at ease with her life. She was nothing like Bella who was always tense, always worried about closing the next big deal. Even when she was alone in her condo at night, she was working. Bella couldn't think of a time when she wasn't putting a new deal together or making new contacts. Quiet moments didn't exist in Bella's life and she wasn't sure she could handle them if they did.

"You're so calm about all of this. I'd be going nuts twenty-four/seven."

Jaycee shrugged. "I'm used to it. I have asthma."

"What?"

"Yeah, it runs in my family. I had it when we were kids."

"I never noticed."

"I was good at hiding it. My symptoms didn't get worse until after you left. I think not having my best friend around to laugh with got me down and made me more susceptible to my allergies."

Jaycee quickly began to chuckle, as if what she'd said had been teasing instead of what was likely the truth.

Bella was stunned. She had been so distraught over leaving and how it was affecting her, she never thought how it affected her friends. She never gave their feelings a second thought. All her angst and torment over leaving had been about her and what she was going through and never did she think about what the separation had done to Jaycee or Dusty…or Travis.

Jaycee continued. "That's the thing about divorce. All the kids suffer no matter who moves away. You may have moved on from us, but we never moved on from you."

"And all this time, I assumed…" Bella leaned back in her chair. "It doesn't matter what I assumed. You were hurting as much as I was."

Jaycee's face went serious, creases formed on her forehead and her eyes were moist with emotion.

"Maybe more. You went off to a big city while I stayed right here surrounded by our memories. One day we were hanging out in the school yard and the next day I was alone. You had distractions. I had the same school and no best friend. You and Travis were my only friends. If it wasn't for him, I don't know how I would have made it through. Yeah, he's a little hokey, but he's got a heart as big as this whole state. And he loves kids. He'll probably have a whole house-full like the rest of the Grangers."

Bella didn't have time in her busy schedule for anyone or anything. She couldn't even take care of a goldfish, let alone a child. It could never work out with Travis, she knew that now.

Still, whenever she thought about their lovemaking, she had to take a deep breath to calm the thrill that shot through her.

"So tell me, has Travis dated anyone seriously?"

"Not really. He dates a lot of girls, but they never last long. He only has one love and that's you. Everybody knows it."

"We're not right for each other. We live in two different worlds."

She smiled. "Temporarily, but if you love each other, it all seems to work out."

"I don't love…Travis." His name caught in her throat.

"See, that right there. That little hitch when you say his name. That's love, pure and simple."

Whether or not she loved Travis didn't matter now. She simply wanted to assure herself that he'd be fine without her, just as she knew she'd be fine without him. Still, she had one more question that had always plagued her when she was a teen.

"Did you two ever date?"

Jaycee cringed, then shivered as if the whole idea of dating Travis was somehow revolting. "We tried one summer when we were around sixteen, but it didn't go past the first awkward kiss. Travis and me are more like brother and sister. It ended up being too weird. Even when we kissed, and you know those Granger boys are the best kissers in Idaho, I couldn't stop giggling."

Bella's eyebrows went up and the two women chuckled.

Jaycee continued, thankfully she didn't seem to notice the blush now heating up Bella's face. "Anyway, it was way too strange. Both of us finally agreed to be friends, and it was the best decision we ever made. Besides, even back then, I knew he was in love with you and he'd wait forever for you to come back to Briggs."

Bella refused to believe that could possibly be true. She took a few sips of her yummy coffee, put the cup back down on the table and looked at Jaycee to see if she was telling a fat one. She could always see right through her. "Travis couldn't possibly be carrying a torch for that many years. I think he's in love with the idea of me as a kid, but the grown-up me is someone he can't relate to."

Jaycee leaned in across the table, lowered her chin and whispered, "You've kissed him, haven't you?"

Bella didn't want to admit anything about the tryst so she avoided looking directly at Jaycee. "Me? Whatever gave you that impression?"

"Some things never change. You're lobster-red, plus you won't look at me. A sure sign you're hiding the truth. Come on. Give."

Bella leaned in, feeling as if they were back in grade school sharing a secret. "Okay, yes, we kissed."

Bella's phone beeped with a text message and she discreetly pulled it out of her purse. It was Mr. Footloose telling her she had a deal. The piano was back in the lobby, unscathed.

She excused herself with Jaycee and texted back that she'd be there to sign the paperwork in twenty minutes. He agreed to wait.

When she looked back up, Jaycee asked, "Did you sleep with him?"

The question caught her by surprise. Bella was never the kind of woman to kiss and tell. It wasn't in her nature. She really frowned on people who did that. Spilling the details of a love affair with someone else was definitely not part of her makeup. "Yes, and it was everything I always dreamed it would be, but now everything is complicated."

"And that means you're not staying." Jaycee pushed her cup away and folded her arms across her chest. "I thought maybe… It doesn't matter."

Her reaction made Bella smile. "Of course you and I will still be best friends. That's a given. Maybe you and your family can come to Chicago someday for a visit. I'll show you all the sights. It's a great city. You'll love it."

Jaycee uncrossed her arms and some of the tension

drained from her face. "What about Travis? He's a cowboy. Cowboys and big cities don't mix."

"Just because I slept with Travis doesn't mean I'm now glued to his side." Bella sat back thinking her time with Travis was simply another encounter with a man, albeit an amazing, magnificent, exciting man, an encounter nonetheless. "It was just sex. Nothing more."

Though she knew their lovemaking was so much more, she couldn't say it out loud or she'd have to honestly consider staying. And that was completely out of the question.

Jaycee sat back in her chair and mimicked Bella's pose. "If that's how you need to rationalize it, go right ahead. It's your life, honey. Still, I think you should know he stopped by earlier today to visit with Georgie. While he was here, he spilled that you're leaving tonight. That you sold all the furniture inside the inn, even your dad's piano. The look on his face said it all. He's devastated. I tried to explain that Chicago is your home, but it didn't sit well with him. I think he might do something rash."

Bella blanched. Her heart raced. Fear clouded her mind. "Rash, like what?"

"Whoa, sweetie. Nothing outrageous. While he was talking to me, he kept pulling on his beard. He's probably going to shave it off before Christmas in retribution for losing you again. Maybe you should talk to him before you leave. Ease him down slowly."

Bella couldn't see Travis again. Not now. Not after she'd hardened her emotions and was back in business where she belonged. Besides, she was running late already and still had to pick up her dad at the inn. No, that was Travis's decision to shave off his beard and not her place to try to convince him otherwise, even though she thought the whole Cowboy Santa was just about the cutest and sweetest part of Travis she'd ever known.

"I don't have time to talk him down, Jaycee. My flight leaves out of Jackson in less than three hours. I have a meeting in Chicago in the morning."

"But it's Christmas Eve tomorrow."

"It's just another day in business."

"Is that how you feel?"

Bella paused before admitting, "I used to, but not so much anymore."

"Then stay."

She stood, wanting the conversation to end. "It's the biggest real-estate deal I've ever brokered. I have to go."

Jaycee shook her head. "That's too bad. With a man like Travis, he may never grow another beard again."

TRAVIS HELD THE razor close to his neck, contemplating his next move. Ever since he'd hit puberty he'd grown a beard for Christmas, bleaching it pure white a few days before the main event. At first his family thought he was taking things too far, then after the third year, they all came to accept it. When his brothers started having kids Travis found a red cowboy hat in a thrift shop in Boise and decided to become Cowboy Santa. His nieces and nephews loved it and before he knew what was happening, he was turning up at Valley Hospital with a sack full of toys. As the years passed his reputation grew and soon, nearly everyone in town came to expect Cowboy Santa to pay them a visit if they were in the hospital.

Then about five years ago, Travis came across an old beat-up sleigh in a barn sale out on Highway 22. Once he'd cleaned it up, spent hours repairing it, then had it painted bright red, he'd known for certain he'd have to buy the right team to pull it. He came across Rio and Wildfire at an auction right outside of Cody, Wyoming, and he knew they completed his Cowboy Santa image.

But now everything had changed.

Not only was he losing Bella once again, but he would be losing a man who was just as much of a father to him as Dodge. How could he celebrate Christmas without Nick? Without Dream Weaver Inn? Without Bella?

He lathered up his beard once again and readied the razor. This time he was determined to go through with it, determined to end his foolish yearly hype of everything Christmas. He was a grown man now. Christmas was for kids, and parents who had kids. It was not for a single guy, and especially not something a cowboy should be getting all excited about. He wondered if any of the iconic cowboys of bygone eras had celebrated Christmas with such enthusiasm. There was absolutely no evidence that any of them had.

Cowboy Santa! Who thought that one up?

He had, and it was just plain childish.

It was time he grew up. Time he acted like a man. Time he let go of his childhood.

With a steady hand he took the first swipe, making a dent in his white whiskers. The vision of a bare spot under his chin sent a chill through him as he pictured the faces of his nieces and nephews looking as sad as hounds losing a trail because Cowboy Santa was clean shaven. What kind of a Santa could he be without his beard?

"A stupid one, that's what."

What was he thinking? Who cared if any of his favorite classic cowboys liked Christmas or if any of them ever wore a red cowboy hat? And just because Bella Biondi had turned into Ms. Scrooge didn't mean he had to, as well. If she refused to embrace her true emotions and refused to accept his love, that didn't mean he had to suddenly do an about-face. Christmas was in his soul, she'd taught him that, and even though she no longer cared about the holiday or about him or for that matter, about her dad and everything she grew up with and had loved, didn't mean he had to give it up, as well. He loved Bella with all his heart, would do anything for her, but he had to draw the line at shaving off his beard.

He leaned over the sink and washed off his face, stored the razor back where it belonged in his medicine cabinet. He was about to walk out of the bathroom, proud of his manly decision to continue his Christmas tradition when he noticed a pair of red gloves on the floor next to the tub, half hidden under a bath towel. At first he thought they were his. He'd worn red gloves the previous night, but his gloves were in the mud room.

If they weren't his gloves, they had to be Bella's.

He reached down and picked them up, turning each one over in his hands. Not only were they red, but each finger had a tiny face sewn on, a Santa, a few elves, and Rudolf with his bright red nose. They were the cutest gloves he'd ever seen. His niece Scout would love them, but they weren't Scout's gloves, they were Bella's.

"Ms. Scrooge wears puppet gloves?" He shook his head in amazement. "The girl is just a case of misdirected bluster."

Chapter Ten

Bella hadn't seen her dad since the previous day when he'd been playing his piano, sitting on the bench next to his brown-haired beauty, Audrey. And like déjà vu, they were once again sitting in the exact same positions, singing a Christmas carol. Only this time the lobby was completely empty. Not one other person was around, and every stick of furniture, carpeting, pictures, drapes, trinkets and Christmas decorations were gone, as if they'd never been there. As if her childhood had never happened, and her dad had never run Dream Weaver Inn.

The starkness of the aftermath was shocking. She'd expected to have a reaction to seeing the inn completely empty, but nothing had prepared her for this. The empty room brought up many memories she'd managed to forget long ago. Now, seeing the room like this, they were digging up her emotional stockpile, which she didn't want dismantled.

Especially today when she was heading back to Chicago to sign off on the sale.

She had called her dad, but he hadn't picked up. He seemed to have another place to stay he liked more than his inn. She couldn't blame him. Even Bella didn't like seeing it this way.

She'd left him a message to please meet her at the inn telling him they would leave from there for the flight out of Jackson to Chicago. Her rented truck would be returned to the affiliate rental agency in Jackson. That made her life easier. She was planning on meeting with TransGlobal bright and early as planned, knowing the deal would cause her a mountain of paperwork she'd have to process on Christmas day, and possibly a few days after that. Her assistant would take care of a lot of it after Christmas vacation, but Bella knew she'd have to be in the office on Christmas to get everything ready for her. The office was usually open during the week between Christmas and New Year's.

She intended to get her dad to Tampa as soon as she could book him a flight out of Chicago. The sooner he could get settled, the better she'd feel about the whole move and he'd begin to make friends and adjust to his new surroundings. She would have liked to help him move in, but there wasn't any time for that now. She'd plan a nice long visit sometime in February or March to make up for that.

A smooth rendition of "Oh Holy Night" echoed through the now empty inn, giving Bella a chill. The harmony between her dad and Audrey sounded well practiced. Another reason for Bella to doubt the friend theory.

And why was Audrey there, anyway? Bella thought the entire scene was rather curious. They didn't notice Bella, so she was able to watch them, sitting together, looking as if there was no one else in the entire world but the two of them enjoying a song. They each knew all the words, and how they looked at each other, smiled at each other, and chuckled whenever someone hit a wrong note Bella knew positively this was much more than a friendship.

Her dad spotted her and stopped playing.

"Hi, Dad," she said, her voice echoing from across the room. "Audrey."

"Bella, we've been waiting for you, sweetheart," her dad said, his voice low and heavy.

She didn't like how that sounded. "We don't have much time, Dad."

"I have something to say. But first, why is the piano still here? Isn't it part of the sale to TransGlobal?"

"I'm having it shipped to Florida for you."

"Thanks, but that's what I want to talk to you about."

"Can it wait until we're in the truck? We don't want to miss our flight."

He stood. "No, it can't. It's about the flight."

Audrey stood, taking his hand in hers and they walked toward Bella who was now leaning on the empty front desk for support. Touching the desk made her think of checking in and suitcases, which her dad didn't seem to have ready and waiting.

"Where are your bags, Dad? Your things?"

"My things are at Audrey's place in Jackson. Moved most of my belongings there a few days ago."

They stood in front of her now. Audrey holding on to her dad's arm. A fashionably modest-sized diamond ring prominent on her left ring finger. Bella's stomach tightened.

"Bella, I won't be going with you. Audrey and I are getting married and I'm moving to Jackson to help run her inn. We had planned on selling her inn in favor of this one, but, well…I'm sorry to disappoint you. I've thought long and hard about this. I can't live in Orlando."

"Tampa."

"Whatever. I can't live in Florida."

Her dad was doing it again. Staying while she left.

"But we've had this all planned. We're finally going to be able to see each other more often, spend time with each other. You would give that up for…for…her?"

Bella pointed to Audrey, and at the very moment she brought her finger up in the air, she realized her dad was serious. If he hadn't left fifteen years ago to be with her mom, he certainly wouldn't be leaving now. This part of the world had a hold on him that was unshakeable, and no one, not even his own daughter could break that bond.

He walked closer to Bella, letting Audrey's hand go. "Bella, I love you very much, but you have your own life to live and unfortunately it's not here in this valley. I can't live anywhere else, and I don't want to do it without Audrey by my side. I'm in love with her, and as amazing as it seems, she's in love with me."

Audrey took a couple steps closer and held her dad's hand. "You can come and visit us anytime, Bella. We'd love to have you. It's a lovely inn. I think you'll enjoy it. Please don't leave angry. Some things you can't plan. They just happen and when they do you have to hold on tight. They may never come your way again."

Bella had heard enough. Her insides shook from her disappointment, not to mention the hassle of owning an empty condo in Tampa. She didn't even like Florida! Way too hot and muggy in the summer. Worse than

Chicago and she could barely deal with Chicago in the summer.

"Congratulations. I'm sure you'll both be very happy. Consider the piano a wedding present. Now if you don't mind, I have a plane to catch."

She turned away before the waterworks could start and stormed out without so much as a hug.

By THE TIME Bella boarded the plane to take her to Chicago, she felt completely drained. Not only did the empty first class seat next to her remind her of how badly she'd failed with her dad, but she was missing Travis more than she wanted to admit. And what was even crazier—she was missing Briggs and they hadn't even taxied down the runway yet.

Bella had booked a flight with one short layover in Denver getting into Chicago a few minutes past midnight, making it officially Christmas Eve. The irony was too much for her to cope with and she found herself tearing up every other minute.

The female attendant with a kind face, brown, shoulder-length hair and a warm smile offered her a tissue and a magazine.

"Thanks," Bella told her eagerly taking both.

"Going home for Christmas?" the attendant asked.

"Leaving," Bella said, her voice catching in her throat as tears streamed down her face. "I don't even like Christmas."

The attendant handed her another tissue. "It's a tough holiday when you're alone."

"It never bothered me before. Matter of fact, I like being alone on Christmas."

She couldn't help but let out a sob. The attendant left, but then returned with a full box of tissues.

Bella accepted the box and held it tight against her chest. "Thank you."

"You're welcome. Please fasten your seat belt, we're about to take off."

That only brought on more tears.

Bella didn't understand where all this emotion was coming from. She never cried. She prided herself on never getting emotional. It was the one thing that she'd learned in business, never to get emotional. Men saw it as a weakness, and women saw it as an opening to grab your position. She knew this for a fact because she'd stolen several promotions from weak women who cried over the silliest of things.

And right now her crying was plain silly. She fastened her seat belt, sat up straight, took a couple deep breaths, slowly letting them out, and got herself under control…sort of. At least enough so that after takeoff she pushed the seat back as far as it would go, closed her eyes and kept repeating: "I like being alone on Christmas. I like being alone on Christmas. I like being…"

The brown-haired attendant nudged Bella once they were on the ground. "Ms. Biondi, you have to wake up now."

When Bella opened her eyes and looked around, the entire plane was empty except for the flight crew who stood at the front of the plane, chatting. There were four of them, two pilots, an older woman with white hair and a tall male attendant. They each wore a Santa hat and one of the pilots sported a white beard that came down to his upper chest. Bella had never seen facial hair on a pilot before and thought he looked odd, especially with a beard that long.

"Sorry," Bella explained. "I can't believe I slept through the entire flight."

"Sometimes that happens," the brown-haired attendant said. "Especially this time of year when everyone is so exhausted from shopping, partying and late-night hours."

The attendant leaned over the chair and looked right at Bella, as if she was waiting for an answer. Bella focused in on her face, and was startled to see how much she looked exactly like her dad's fiancée, Audrey.

"You look like someone I know."

"I know. I look like Audrey."

"What?"

"You're exhausted from shopping and having too much fun, right?"

Bella couldn't think straight. Her mind seemed muddled as she tried to answer the question. "No. I didn't shop for anything or party. I don't celebrate Christmas."

The entire crew turned to stare at her, a look of horror on their collective faces.

"You don't celebrate Christmas?" they said in unison.

"No," Bella repeated, her voice shaky.

There was a unilateral gasp as their attention focused in on Bella.

"We have a strict code," the bearded pilot said. "No one gets on our flight who doesn't celebrate Christmas. You should have told us this information before we took off. Didn't you fill out the paperwork?"

"What paperwork? No one gave me anything to fill out."

"She kept changing her itinerary. Maybe that's why she didn't get the paperwork filled out in time," one of the male attendants said. He was busy looking down at a clipboard, shaking his head. Now that Bella took a good look at him, he had a striking resemblance to Mr. Footloose.

"How did you know...?"

"This is a total breach of security," the older woman announced.

"This flight is strictly for people who celebrate Christmas. No exceptions," the bearded pilot stated in no uncertain terms.

"You can't impose a law like that. It's un-American!"

The crew came marching toward her as panic tightened Bella's chest. She needed to get out of there, fast. She grabbed her purse, pushed Attendant Audrey aside and ran past the first-class curtain, down the empty coach aisle and out the side door, taking the metal stairs two at a time and ran smack into Travis. He was all decked out in his Cowboy Santa outfit, but this time his beard was longer, much longer, and he glowed from twinkling white lights that encircled his hat, went down his arms and legs and were scattered throughout his beard.

She was delighted to see him and gave him a tight hug, thinking he could tell her what was going on. "Travis, I'm so glad you're here. You won't believe what happened on that plane."

"Bella, we've been waiting for you," he said, his voice raspy and deep.

At once Bella found herself in Belly Up, surrounded by her childhood classmates. Milo Gump tended bar while his wife, Amanda, busied herself carving a life-size snow Santa in the center of the room. Amanda turned and waved just as the little girl Bella had evicted from Dream Weaver Inn appeared from behind the Santa, carrying a huge snowball in each hand. The little girl fired them straight at snow Santa, then ran up to what was left of him and began kicking him in the shins.

"Wait! Stop!" Bella cried out, but the little girl acted as if she didn't hear Bella and didn't stop until the Santa was in complete ruin.

"She can't hear you," Cowboy Santa Travis said. "No one can."

"But you can hear me."

He smirked. "I'm different. Come with me." He took her hand and suddenly they were standing in his Christmas loft at his house.

"I love this room," Bella told him, feeling safe and warm. Her trunk lay open in the corner, only her things were no longer inside. Instead dollhouse furniture was piled up, dollhouse furniture that looked exactly like the furniture from Dream Weaver Inn.

She turned away, not wanting to see it.

"Just watch," Cowboy Santa Travis ordered, pointing down to the bedroom.

Jaycee padded into the master bedroom. She looked at least eight months pregnant, her stomach big and round under a bright red dress. She walked over to the closet, slid open the door and searched for something inside.

Travis, wearing a cream-colored sweater, jeans and black cowboy boots walked up behind her, leaned over and nibbled on her ear. "How do you feel, babe?"

Bella turned to see Cowboy Santa Travis still standing beside her. "I don't understand. How can you be up here with me and down there with Jaycee at the same time?"

"Christmas magic."

"I don't believe in Christmas."

He guffawed. "I know."

Jaycee turned to face the other Travis. She seemed to be glowing from the soft lights on the Christmas tree up in the loft. "Happy. I have an inkling our baby will be born Christmas Day, making it our best Christmas ever." Then he kissed her with all the passion he'd kissed Bella with the night before.

"Nooo!" Bella yelled lunging forward, but Cowboy Santa Travis grabbed her waist and wouldn't let go. "No! You love me, not her!"

"Ms. Biondi. Ms. Biondi. It's time to wake up."

Bella jolted up straight and her eyes flew open to see the brown-haired attendant standing over her. Bella instantly drew back, wanting to get away from her. "I love Christmas. Honest I do. I'll fill out the paperwork. Just don't make me go back there."

The attendant smiled. "We've landed in Chicago. You were sleeping and I didn't have the heart to wake you, but you have to get off the plane now."

Bella scrambled out of her seat. The plane was empty, and the crew stood up front, but this time the pilots were clean shaven and neither one of them held a clipboard. Blinking a couple times to get her focus, Bella regained her bearings and realized she had, in fact, been dreaming. "I am so sorry."

"Not a problem. I know how stressful this time of year can be. All that shopping and partying is enough to make anyone tired."

Bella's eyes went wide as she grabbed her purse and

rushed off the plane from the first class exit. For the first time since she was a kid, she knew exactly what she wanted and what she needed to do to get it.

TRAVIS DIDN'T KNOW much about Chicago, and frankly didn't care. Big cities weren't his thing. He was a small-town Western boy through and through, but if Bella had insisted on flying back to Chicago without her Santa gloves, then Travis had no choice but to return them in person.

At least that was what he told himself as he sat on the small jet at the Jackson airport. His brother Colt had driven him to the airport landing with barely enough time to make it to the main terminal. He was the last one to board before they closed the doors.

He didn't catch any sleep on the plane, plagued with concern over how Bella would react to seeing him in her town. And it didn't help that he'd scored a middle seat between a guy who snored like a bullfrog on a lily pad and a woman who insisted on eating chips and nuts and everything else she could crunch for the entire flight.

When the plane finally landed he thought his troubles were over until he stood out in the frigid cold, trying to scare down a cab in the middle of the night, with the wind making his life miserable. He wore his favorite black beaver hat to keep his head warm, but it was no match for Chicago's relentless wind. His bright idea to return Bella's Christmas gloves in person ranked right up there with getting his fingers caught in a barn door.

Travelers came and went as friends and families picked up the wandering groups curbside. Travis tried to hail a cab several times, but each time he thought he'd secured one someone else would jump in before he had the chance to open a door.

Soon it began to snow and not the pretty cornflake snow he loved, but the blizzard type that blew in his face and felt like so many tiny needles. Snow soon collected on the sidewalk, on the street, on his beard, his hat and on his shoulders. If he stood out there much longer he was sure the authorities would come and cart him away for being some kind of threat to national security.

And right when Travis thought he'd never get a cab, he noticed the woman getting into a black Town Car about thirty feet up the sidewalk. He instantly knew those clothes, and that lovely hair, and that haughty little knit hat. It was Bella.

He called out her name several times and ran toward her, pulling his bag behind him, but apparently she didn't hear him due to all the racket coming from the planes flying overhead and the cars and the rush of people all vying for cabs or shuttles. As she drove past him he waved frantically, but when she glanced in his direction, some guy in a bright green jacket chose that exact moment to walk right in front of him.

In the next second her Town Car blended into the tangle of other vehicles leaving the airport making it impossible for him to spot her car.

It was times like these when Travis wished he'd taken the few seconds while Bella was in Briggs to get her dang phone number. It would have made his life so much easier. He'd tried calling Nick for the number, but Nick wasn't the kind of guy who carried his cell phone wherever he went. It was more of an emergency type of gadget for him and most of the time he left it in his truck or on his dresser, which he didn't have anymore. Travis knew about him moving in with Audrey instead of moving to Tampa to play golf. A good decision, but now that he had a woman on his mind, there was no telling if Nick would ever be interested in his cell phone again. He didn't know anything about Audrey's inn or he'd call over there. Heck, he didn't even know Audrey's last name.

Travis felt a slight tug on his coat and looked down to see a boy with big dark eyes staring up at him. He wore a bulky black leather jacket, mini black biker boots, black mittens and a thick black cap.

"Are you a real cowboy?" the little boy asked in a voice as high pitched as a canary. His mom stood a few feet away, watching his every move while she wrangled several suitcases and bags.

Travis smiled over at her and nodded. She returned the gesture.

"I sure am."

"Where's your horse?"

"In Idaho."

"Is that far?"

"Yes. It's a whole lotta far."

"Is it on another planet?"

"Not that far."

"Do you miss your horse?"

"Yes."

"Maybe you can borrow one from my daddy. He's got plenty of horses. I've never seen them though. They hide in his engine."

"That's a different kind of horse."

And at that exact moment, a bright orange Mustang Cobra roared up and parked curbside. A tall lanky guy jumped out dressed entirely in black leather.

"Daddy!" the boy yelled, running for the driver's arms. They looked exactly alike not only in dress but in facial features. The vision gave new meaning to the term "little man."

In less time than it took for Travis to move out of their path, the dad had his family in the car along with their bags, driving off with more horsepower than an entire team of Clydesdales could ever muster.

"And that there's an example of city horsepower," Travis said aloud just as a blast of wind and snow blew his hat off and rolled it down the sidewalk.

BELLA THOUGHT FOR sure she'd seen Travis waving to her in front of the airport. She wanted the driver to stop, but the traffic made that impossible. Then she thought about circling the airport to make sure it wasn't him, but dismissed the idea as the airport exit loomed in front of them. She figured the vision had to be remnants of her dream. There was absolutely no way Travis Granger would have flown to Chicago on Christmas Eve. He probably had a mountain of Christmas festivities planned and Travis was most definitely not the sort of guy to leave anyone in the lurch, let alone not enjoy Christmas in his hometown.

It was merely wishful thinking on her part. After everything she'd done, the things she'd said and how badly she treated him and her dad, she wouldn't blame either one of them if they never spoke to her or trusted her again.

Still, she was going to try to make it up to them.

Never mind feeling sorry for herself, or dwelling on what she would have done differently, she settled back, opened her briefcase, booted up her laptop and went to work as the driver steered onto the Kennedy Expressway.

She sent her dad an urgent email detailing her plan to swap out his inn for Audrey's inn. Bella would take care of the details with TransGlobal, but she needed signatures from both of them if this deal had any chance of going through when she met with the executives in the morning. Bella knew her future depended on her father's response in order for her to begin to put this new proposal together. She could hardly contain herself after she hit send, realizing she'd have to wait for his response.

Time seemed to stand still while she counted off the minutes, knowing full well that the chances of her dad being anywhere near his computer or phone were pretty remote.

She peered out the window at the endless stream of cars filled with people she didn't know and would never know as they rushed by her. She longed for the familiarity of Briggs. Fear began to take hold as the time ticked by and her dad didn't respond. If he wouldn't go for it, she had no idea what plan B looked like.

At this point, selling her dad's inn to TransGlobal was out of the question. She'd made a mess of everything and this was her one shot to make it right.

Her laptop pinged indicating she had a new email and her heart skipped a beat. She quickly opened it and wanted to do a happy dance right there on the back seat. Her dad and Audrey had agreed to the deal. She immediately wrote back telling him she'd be in touch early in the morning and they promised to keep Nick's phone nearby and wait for her call. She collected Audrey's stats on her inn and for the rest of the ride into the city Bella worked on the new proposal, completely excited about this venture.

She knew she would have to pull an all-nighter to get everything ready for the next day. She was prepared to give TransGlobal an offer they couldn't possibly refuse even if it meant she would have to take a significant cut to her commission, which she would gladly do.

With that set in motion, she pulled out the card Dusty Spenser had given her and sent him an email, asking about the house on Main Street in Briggs that Jaycee had told her about. She decided to purchase the house for Jaycee and cover any closing costs so she and her family could move in sooner rather than later. It was the least she could do for her very best friend in the entire world. Besides, she'd be selling that condo in Orlando. Tampa.

Whatever.

Bella didn't count on a speedy reply to her email, figuring Dusty was probably asleep. She'd call him in the morning before meeting with TransGlobal. But within seconds after she hit send, he answered.

Way too thrilled about this idea, she decided to call him instead of sending emails back and forth.

"I have a favor to ask," she said before he could say hello.

"Anything for you, darlin'."

His agreeable voice put a smile on her face.

"As I said in the email, there's a house on Main Street in Briggs that's going to come on the market soon. Do you know who owns it?"

"Sure do. The Orloffs want to sell their sweet little house. Movin' to San Diego with a brand new company. It won't be up for sale until around March, though. You and Travis in need of some courtin' time? You plannin' on movin' back to Briggs?"

"I live in Chicago, Dusty. It's where my job is located. Travis is still in Briggs."

There was an awkward pause, then he said, "I'm sure he wants to be in Chicago right there with you."

"He's a cowboy, and a cowboy belongs on a ranch, not in a crowded city."

"And you're a cowgirl. What the heck are you doin' in that noisy city? You used to be able to ride and rope better than all those Granger boys put together."

"I hung up my spurs a long time ago. Wouldn't know the first thing about it now."

"You can take the cowgirl out of the country, but you can't take the country out of the cowgirl."

"I think I've heard that statement a time or two."

"Hearin' it and believin' it are two different things. No matter where you go, darlin', country's a part of you. Ain't nothin' you can do about it. I don't care how many pairs of city boots you own."

Dusty seemed to know her better than she knew herself.

"In just five minutes, Dusty, you've managed to clarify what's been my core problem for my entire adult life."

She pulled out a tissue from her purse and sponged up the tears that were sliding down her cheeks.

"Shucks, sweetheart, you should'a called me years ago."

"If I hadn't been so stuck on myself, I probably would have. You're a good friend, Dusty, still, after all this time."

"There's no expiration date on friendship."

She chuckled. "No. There sure isn't."

"Glad to help. Now just tell ole' Dusty what else is on your mind."

"I want to buy the Orloff house and I want to give them an offer they…"

"…can't refuse?"

"Exactly."

"You came to the right place, sweetheart. Now tell me, what does a city girl want with a country house?"

"It's not for me. It's for Jaycee."

"Bella, you're a good friend."

"I'm learning."

Chapter Eleven

When Travis finally booked a room for the night he was dog tired. Just flagging down a cab had taken it out of him, especially since it meant he had to stand out in below-zero temperatures, with a wind-chill factor that could freeze a heifer solid before dawn. He'd wanted to go in search of Bella, utilizing all his friends back home to try and find out any information about where she lived or worked, but everyone he'd made contact with came up empty handed. When his head hit the pillow in his fancy room it was going on two in the morning Chicago time and Travis could barely keep his eyes open, let alone think of where Bella might be. He only hoped she was safe and warm.

He tried to make himself comfortable in what seemed like the only room available in the entire city. Fortunately the pretty blonde working the desk seemed to like cowboys and had given him a significant cut in the price, so he took it. He figured it was either give the girl his credit card and book the room or sleep on the street. Neither option seemed worthy of returning a pair of Christmas gloves to a woman who chose her job over his affections, but Travis was now on a mission and nothing short of freezing to death was going to stop him.

He'd taken a long bath in the impressive whirlpool tub wishing like heck that Bella were in that tub with him, and was just settling into his soft bed when his phone rang. Dusty Spenser's picture popped up on the screen.

"What's a cowboy like you doin' in a big city like Chicago?" Dusty asked, his voice sounding friendly. It was exactly what Travis needed after the night he'd been through.

"How'd you know I was here?"

"Half the town knows. Did you see her yet?"

"See who?"

"This is Dusty you're talking to. I've known you since you were old enough to swing a rope. Did you see Bella yet?"

"Yep, but she didn't see me. I tried to get her attention when she drove off in her swanky black car complete with a driver, but she didn't pay me no mind."

Travis yawned and rested his head on the down pillow. Between the puffy mattress and the feather pillow he felt as if he were floating on a cloud and wondered how anybody could sleep under such extravagant conditions.

"That's too bad."

"I think so. What's keeping you up so late, partner?"

"Talkin' to your girl."

"I don't have a girl."

"Yes, you do and she's busy buying houses for her friends."

"What's that supposed to mean?"

"I'll let her tell you."

"You didn't tell her I was here in Chicago, did you?" Travis pushed himself up in bed, his pulse racing. "I mean what if she doesn't want to see me, and you already told her I'm here. She might feel obligated to see me when she really doesn't want to."

"Hold on there, buddy. I didn't tell that girl nothin'."

"So why are you calling me?"

"To give you her addresses. I'm thinkin' you weren't smart enough to get them from Nick before you hopped on that there love plane and flew out to get your girl."

Dusty and Travis had been best friends for a lot of years, and unfortunately Dusty knew all of Travis's good points as well as his bad. Getting the details before he started out on a journey was not one of his strongest attributes.

Travis chuckled and scratched his beard. "That's why we're a good team, buddy. You care about the details while I'm only interested in the big picture."

"You owe me for this one."

"I thought I already owed you."

"You do. This is bigger. I'm savin' your life here with the girl you love."

"Might be, but first we have to see if she feels the same."

"From what I hear, you got a real good chance."

Travis slid out of bed, pacing the floor while he held the phone tight against his ear. "Yeah? What did she say? Anything about me?"

"I don't spread rumors. Do you want her addresses or not?"

Travis sighed and dropped down on the bed, knowing dang well he wasn't going to get anything more out of Dusty.

"Sure. Lay them on me."

TRAVIS ARRIVED AT Bella's company a little after nine the next morning. He knew Bella liked to get a head start on things, so going to her condo would have been a waste of his time. Besides, her condo was several miles away, whereas the company she worked for, Ewing Inc., was within walking distance from his hotel.

It had warmed up and the wind had stopped blowing so his hat stayed on his head and kept him toasty while he trudged through endless drifts of snow. It was one thing when a town like Briggs was snowed under for a day or two, but quite another to see a big city come to a standstill.

The city seemed eerily quiet on this Christmas Eve morning, with no one on the sidewalks except for some last-minute early shoppers and a few brave souls who couldn't make it without their cup of java from the local coffee house. Fortunately, his hotel had provided free coffee—which he'd drank three cups of before stepping one foot out in the cold—along with a blueberry muffin and a mess of scrambled eggs.

Ewing, Inc. was located inside the John Hancock Center, and when Travis made it to the ultramodern black, white and tan reception area asking for Ms. Bella Biondi, the fine-looking woman in her late twenties sitting behind the tall oak desk told him she was in a meeting.

"Do you know how long it will last?" Travis asked as politely as he knew how.

She looked something up on her sleek computer with the thirty inch monitor on her desk. "At least another fifteen minutes."

"Is there someplace I can wait? It's important that I see her."

"Is this business or pleasure?"

"Pure pleasure."

A smile creased the corners of her mouth.

"Are you a family member?"

"In a manner of speaking, yes."

"And what is this concerning?"

"I'm returning something she left behind in Idaho."

"And may I ask what that might be?"

"Me."

Her face turned a bright crimson as she tried to compose herself by tugging on the bottom of her navy suit jacket. "And you are?"

"A restless cowboy."

She snickered. "I still need a name."

"I want it to be a surprise."

She shook her head. "I'm sorry, but I can't let you wait for her without a name."

"Travis Granger."

"Follow me."

He followed her through two oak doors, down a short hallway and into a large office that had to belong to Bella. The young lady told him to help himself to a beverage in the break room down the hall. Then she smiled and left. There were no real telltale signs this was Bella's space except for a small picture of her mom, dad and Bella standing in front of Dream Weaver Inn that sat on a bookshelf behind her desk. Bella couldn't have been more than five years old in the picture and looked about as innocent and happy as a kitten with a ball of string. That was probably the year he first met Bella in school. It was sappy to admit, even to himself, but he remembered that blue-and-white polka-dot dress and how pretty she'd looked in it.

He'd been in love with her even then.

Travis took off his coat and hat and tossed them on a black leather chair, then found the break room for another cup of coffee. As he meandered down the hallway, he noticed a glass wall ahead of him and realized it was probably a conference room. He wondered if Bella's meeting was going on inside as he crept closer. A couple of employees passed him in the hallway and Travis greeted them with a pleasant "Mornin'" but there was no response. Neither of them looked up from whatever was so interesting on their phones.

When he finally walked by the glass wall and peeked inside, he spotted Bella right off, decked out in a gray business suit, high heels, a pink shirt and her dazzling silky hair was pulled back in a sleek bun. The room was overrun with men and women in business wear, each of them sitting around a rectangular table, following along on their sleek laptops. At the head of the table stood Bella, her face intent and serious as she addressed the group. Numbers and a summer shot of Dream Weaver Inn sat on a screen behind her. Every now and then, she'd angle off to the side of the screen and point a red beam at the numbers or the inn.

It all looked practiced and very much like the business world he imagined her working in. Nothing like it existed in Briggs, and he wondered how the heck he would ever fit into Bella's world. What would they talk about? What would they have in common? Even his sister-in-law Maggie with her international marketing business never looked like the view he had before him. She was more into laptop meetings with her customers around the world. She usually wore jeans and a T-shirt or a Western blouse and was barefooted most of the time.

Travis couldn't take his eyes off the spectacle in front of him, everyone listening, nodding at the appropriate times, as if they'd been trained to react on cue. He could hardly breathe as he watched the love of his life soundlessly give a presentation. She looked stately. She looked knowledgeable and in her element.

But most of all, she looked happy.

He finally understood what she'd been trying to tell him about her love for Chicago and her job. As he watched her now, he knew this was where she belonged. Her mom had been right to leave Briggs. She knew what her daughter needed better than Nick or Travis ever could.

The room suddenly erupted with laughter. Apparently Bella had told a joke or said something funny because she was chuckling right along with everyone. Her face beamed with delight as one of the older men stood, buttoned his jacket, walked over to her and shook her hand. Travis guessed her big deal with TransGlobal had been confirmed and Dream Weaver Inn now belonged to a conglomerate.

Mission accomplished.

Bella's face positively glowed as one of those great big wonderful smiles of hers spread across her face. One by one the men and women who'd been sitting around the table walked up to her to shake her hand and she returned the gesture eagerly.

Now he knew for certain that Bella belonged in the world of business and not on a small-town ranch.

Travis wanted to remember her like this whenever he longed for her in his bed, whenever he thought of kissing those full lips, or when he thought of her naked body under his. Just then she gazed at him, but he stepped back before they made eye contact. He quickly retreated down the hallway, picked up his coat and hat and headed to the main lobby.

He'd seen enough.

When he popped through the oak doors and strode for the exit, the receptionist tried to stop him. "Mr. Granger, Ms. Biondi's meeting is over. Don't you want to wait for her?"

"No. Thanks."

He kept walking.

"But I thought you were returning something from Idaho?"

He stopped and turned to face her. "Once again you've got it right. I'm returning myself to Idaho."

"Is there anything I should tell Ms. Biondi?"

Travis hesitated. He had come all this way, the least he could do was leave her dang gloves, not that she'd ever want them or consider wearing them dressed in her business suit, and slicked back hair. They were as corny as that life-size Santa he'd insisted on putting up on the roof at the inn every year.

He pulled the gloves out of his coat pocket, anyway, walked back and handed them to her. She didn't take them. Instead she stared down at them as if they were as foreign to her as a pair of cowboy boots on a duck.

"Is there a message?"

She gingerly took the gloves and dropped them on her desk.

"Yes, tell her it's cold outside and I thought she might need these."

It cost Bella a full five minutes to shake everyone's hand, grab her hat and coat and rush out to the lobby.

"Was there by any chance a cowboy here looking for me?" Bella asked the new receptionist, as she barreled into the lobby sliding on her coat and trying to deal with both her purse and her briefcase. She had left a message for the receptionist that if a Travis Granger came calling, to please escort him to her office immediately.

Once again, exactly like what had happened at the airport, she thought she'd seen Travis. This time he'd been standing right outside the conference room. She had wanted to go after him, but couldn't get out of the room fast enough due to everyone congratulating her. The deal had gone through, and Bella stood to make well over seven figures…which any other time would have made her ecstatic. More importantly she had managed to save Dream Weaver Inn and get Audrey a great price for hers.

A couple of weeks ago, the deal would have sent her spinning with euphoria.

But not today.

What sent a jolt through her, what sent her pulse into the stratosphere, and gave her goose bumps was the thought that Travis Granger might actually have followed her to Chicago.

That notion sent her heart reeling. She could only hope it was true.

She'd already changed out of her heels and into the boots she'd bought in Briggs, pulled out her knit hat to slip on her head, and a warm scarf for her neck. Unfortunately, she hadn't been able to find her leather gloves in her apartment so her hands had been cold ever since she'd stepped off the plane. Chicago was running well below zero with a wind chill that could freeze your lungs if you stayed outside for more than fifteen minutes, or at least that was how it felt.

"Yes, Travis Granger, the cowboy with the strange white beard, left a few minutes ago."

Bella's heart beat hard against her chest. She was so excited she could hardly stand still for another second.

"I can't believe he's here. Did he say where he was going?" Bella headed for the bank of elevators right outside the lobby.

"Not exactly, but he did leave these for you. He said he thought you might need them."

Bella couldn't make out what she was holding at first. Then as she approached the desk, Bella realized the new, absolutely amazing and wonderfully gifted receptionist who deserved a raise and a promotion, was holding exactly what Bella needed more than her next breath.

"My puppet gloves! He found my puppet gloves! I thought I'd lost them, but he had them all along."

Bella glided the gloves on her hands, making sure the little faces were facing the right direction. Then she held up all ten fingers and wiggled them around.

The receptionist giggled. "They're different, I'll say that much for them."

"I truly need these gloves. They're the absolute most perfect gloves I've ever worn."

"Whatever you say."

"Did he tell you where he was going? A hotel? A restaurant? Anything?"

"He said he was returning himself to Idaho." She enunciated each word as if she was trying to repeat what Travis had said exactly.

"You, my dear, are brilliant! Thank you. Take the rest of the day off. Matter of fact, take the rest of the year off. Merry Christmas!"

"Thank you," the girl mumbled, but Bella was already out of the lobby.

She just wanted to find Travis, as quickly as she could.

TRAVIS HAD SPENT most of Christmas Eve day wandering around O'Hare airport waiting to get on a flight home. He'd missed the earlier flight because he had to return to the hotel first to pick up his bag, and by the time he finally arrived at the airport, the flight was just taking off.

The next one didn't get him in until almost eight o'clock, and by then he would miss dinner with his family, but at least he'd be home in time to open presents. His mom had always liked to open the adults' presents on Christmas Eve and the kids would open theirs on Christmas morning. At least that had always been the plan, but it never quite worked once he and his brothers were past the age of believing in Santa. In the end, everyone opened their presents on Christmas Eve and it was now a set Granger tradition, one that Travis was not about to miss.

Travis plowed through the busy airport to his gate. On the one hand he was happy to be getting out of Chicago, but on the other, he was torn up over leaving Bella behind. He thought they could work something out, meet half way, come to some sort of agreement, but when he'd seen her in her element he knew there was no happy medium. She was all about the city and he was all about the country. It'd be impossible for them to meet in the middle.

Not now.

Not ever.

He somehow knew it right from the start, on that first day when he saw her strutting her city boots up the front stairs of Dream Weaver Inn, but he simply couldn't accept the reality…a shortcoming on his part, no doubt.

Now as he leaned against a pillar waiting for his flight to board in the crowded gate area, and stared at the faces of all the people going home for Christmas, he felt about as out of place as a mule surrounded by thoroughbreds.

As he searched the faces, he couldn't help but make up little stories in his head about where they were all going and who they were meeting.

College students trying to make it home in time for Christmas, aunts and uncles eager to see their family, a soldier going home for the first time in months surprising his family and a teenage boy flying across the country to be with his dad or mom on Christmas.

Everyone flying into love.

Everyone except Travis who was flying away from his true love, his soul mate, his one and only.

When he boarded the plane, the sadness he felt in his heart was almost too much. He knew he would never be the same now that Bella was out of his life for good this time.

The flight home was almost empty, so no one sat next to Travis. He slept for most of it and when he awoke it was time to deplane.

His brother Colt picked him up at the airport in his SUV.

"Everybody's waiting for you before they open their presents," Colt said once he and Travis were on the road back to Briggs from the airport in Jackson. The weather wasn't right for flying so this time Colt drove. "I take it things didn't work out like you hoped they would."

"Didn't even get to talk to her," Travis said feeling worn out by the entire experience. "Taught me a big lesson though."

"What's that?"

"That childhood-sweetheart stuff is a nice memory, nothing else. I've been carrying around a torch for a girl who doesn't exist. Well, I'm done with all that. It's time for me to move on."

"You might want to wait a spell before you make up your mind on Bella."

"Nothing to wait for. She's citified and there isn't anything this tired ole cowboy can do to change it. Plus, I learned that me and a big city don't get along. Not my style. Wait until I tell you about a kid I met who thought his dad kept real live horses under the hood of his Mustang."

Colt chuckled. "You can tell me all about it later. Right now we have to stop in town."

Travis yawned. "I'm really beat. You mind if we go straight to the ranch?"

"Can't. I made a promise to some people."

"Fine, but I hope it's nothing I have to participate in."

"You just lie back, little brother, and I'll wake you when we get there."

Travis did just that. He slid down and rested his head on the back of the headrest, covering his face with his hat and immediately drifted off. The last two days had worn out his spirit and sleep was the only solution to get it spruced up again.

"Come on, Travis, wake up. We're here," Colt said from somewhere off in a distance.

Travis pushed himself up in the seat. "I thought you said you had to stop in town."

"We are in town. Now shake off that sleep and get your tired body up and out of the car."

When Travis finally looked around Colt had parked in front of Dream Weaver Inn. Travis took one look at the inn and had to shake his head to get the cobwebs out, either that or he was dreaming.

The place was awash in Christmas. Lights and garland adorned the exterior, and even those dang N-O-E-L letters sat in the front yard. Travis could see his family and friends milling around inside through the windows.

"What's going on, big brother? Is this some kind of joke? Am I dreaming?"

"Let's go inside and you tell me."

Travis followed Colt up the walkway as the sound of Nick's voice echoed with a verse of "Jingle Bells."

"This can't be happening," Travis yelled to Colt, but Colt ignored him and kept crunching through the icy snow to get to the front door.

When Colt opened the door, everyone stopped what they were doing and yelled, "Merry Christmas!"

It was all Travis could do to keep his eyes from watering, especially when he spotted Bella in the back of the room, waving those crazy, puppet-gloved hands at him wearing the prettiest little smile he'd ever seen. Janet and the rest of the staff were there along with Dusty and his cute wife, Dora, who wore a grin so big Travis thought her cheeks might hurt. Jaycee, her husband and all her children, including little Georgie, who looked about as happy as a peacock showing off its feathers, surrounded best friend Bella, while baby Bella pulled on her mama's blue shirt, wanting to be fed, no doubt.

Milo stood in the back next to his wife, Amanda, and even Harry B. Truman sat on the sofa, a pink scarf around his neck and his little shaggy dog with the pink bows sat curled up on his lap.

Most of the furniture was back in place and an even bigger decorated tree sat in the corner of the room.

Nick threw him the biggest grin he'd seen on him in years as Audrey toasted Travis with her eggnog mug. All the kids were yelling and clapping, even tiny Loran was in on the game.

Travis wanted to burst with joy, but instead he walked right over to Bella, wrapped her in his arms and kissed her with all the force of a hurricane. Her lips felt hot on his mouth as her body melded into his. He kept pulling her in tighter as the chaos of voices mixed with clatter in the room and reached a fever pitch.

Then he momentarily pulled away. "Is it really you?"

Tears filled her eyes as she nodded. "Yes."

"But what about your job? Chicago? And…"

"If you would've hung around I would have told you I swapped out Audrey's inn for my dad's and TransGlobal went for it. As far as my job goes. I quit, or at least I quit working from Chicago. Maggie's agreed to teach me all about working from a remote site, and my boss thinks it's a great idea. But right now, I really need to celebrate Christmas with you, my friends and family."

Travis grinned, knowing that was exactly what she'd needed all along.

"It's time to open presents," Dodge announced, getting everyone to calm down.

Travis felt a pull on his coattail. "Yeah, Uncle Travis, you've got forever to kiss Bella, but we only get one Christmas Eve a year and it's fading mighty fast," Colt's son, Joey said, looking up at him with those big, innocent eyes.

"It sure is," he told Joey, and within moments the room had quieted down, and one by one the pile of presents stacked under and around the newly decorated tree were handed out by Scout, Joey and little Georgie, each now wearing Santa hats.

"This is the best Christmas ever," Bella said.

Travis leaned over and gently brushed her lips with his. "Only because we get to celebrate it together."

"Forever," Bella said, and at once Travis knew she had finally come home to stay.

Epilogue

Bella hadn't been up on a horse in more than fifteen years, and it was about time she tackled her fears.

"You can do this," Travis said as he held the horse steady.

It was a beautiful spring day in the Teton Valley. One of those days when the temperature was perfect, a warm breeze tickled her face, and the entire Granger clan watched from the porch on the main ranch house.

"You can do it, Aunt Bella," Joey yelled.

"Just get on up there," Buddy encouraged.

"He won't bite," Scout said.

Bella hadn't meant for this moment to turn into a family tough-love situation. They'd been getting ready to sit down to their weekly Sunday dinner when Travis had asked her, "So, isn't it about time we went for a ride?"

She knew he hadn't meant in a car.

She'd thought about tackling her fears each time she visited Helen's riding school, but for some reason, she'd never screwed up enough courage to actually ride.

Today, however, all full of herself, she'd boasted how she had no fear of riding if the opportunity presented itself.

"Got Tater all saddled up for you," Travis had said. "He's real gentle."

Tater was Helen's well-trained gelding from her time as a cowboy mounted shooter—a honey-colored Nokota—that Bella had seen Helen ride several times. The animal was like a fine-tuned car that reacted to Helen's every move. If there was ever a horse that was perfect for Bella's first ride, it was Tater.

"You brought over your horse?" Bella had asked Helen.

"Rode him here this morning," Helen answered.

There was no getting out of it this time, so there she was trying to act completely fearless, when her insides were slowly churning.

Travis said, "Where's the fight? If you can't muster up any grit, you'll have to sit on the porch and wait for me, 'cause I'm going for a ride."

He let go of Tater, walked over to a chestnut-colored horse and in less time than it took for Bella to blink he was in the saddle and headed for the trail that ran behind the house.

Without thinking, Bella held on to the reins, making sure the inside one was shorter. Then she grabbed the horn on the saddle with her forward hand, stuck a booted foot in the stirrup, and in one smooth move, she pulled herself up and swung her other leg over Tater's rear end. Cautiously she slowly lowered herself in the saddle. After she made sure the stirrups fit her height, which they did, she gave Tater a gentle nudge and just like that, she had conquered her fear.

Everyone on the porch cheered as she eased Tater into a gentle canter to catch up with Travis. Being horseback after so much time had passed sent a rush of emotion through Bella. The gentle sway of the animal, combined with the open sky, the lush landscape and the breathtaking view of the Teton Mountain Range only made her realize just how blessed she was to once again be living in this beautiful valley.

So much had happened since Christmas that Bella could hardly believe it was real. There were mornings when she'd wake up next to Travis and have to pinch herself to make sure she wasn't dreaming.

They'd gotten married in late April at the inn, with the big shindig reception afterward on the Granger ranch. She and Travis lived at his ranch house now, while her dad and Audrey, who were planning their October wedding, lived at the inn.

Bella helped them out whenever she could, but for the most part, she had decided to take a break from the business world for a while. She wanted to learn how to live at a slower pace, and enjoy the ranch, her hometown, her new family and especially her new husband.

"You look good in the saddle," Travis said once she rode up next to him.

"Did you ever doubt I wouldn't?" she teased.

"Nope. Just took a while."

"I tend to do things at my own speed."

"Fifteen years is a long time to wait."

"But I'm *so* worth it."

They kissed, sending a shiver through her body. When Travis kissed her no matter where they were or how quickly the kiss ended, he always managed to excite her.

He chuckled as he pulled away. "Darlin', that's for dang sure."

He removed his hat, leaned forward in the saddle,

let out a loud yee-ha, and took off like the wind. She wasn't quite sure she could catch up to him, but from where she had come from, nothing would ever get in her way again.

* * * * *

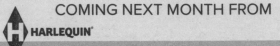

*Looking for more exciting all-American romances
like the one you just read?*

*Read on for an excerpt from
A COWBOY OF HER OWN, part of
THE CASH BROTHERS miniseries,
by Marin Thomas…*

Porter grew quiet for a minute then said, "One day I'm going to buy a ranch."

"Where?"

"I've got my eye on a place in the Fortuna Foothills."

"That's a nice area." Buying property in the foothills would require a large chunk of money, and she doubted a bank would loan it to him.

What if Porter was rustling bulls under Buddy's nose and selling them on the black market in order to finance his dream? As soon as the thought entered her mind, she pushed it away.

"So what do you say?" he said.

"What do I say about what?"

"Having a little fun before we pack it in for the night?"

"It's late. I'm not—"

"Ten o'clock isn't late." When she didn't comment, he said, "C'mon. Let your hair down."

"Are you insinuating that I'm no fun?" she teased, knowing that it was the truth.

"I'm not insinuating. I'm flat out saying it's so."

She'd show him she knew how to party. "Go ahead and stop somewhere."

Two miles later Porter pulled into the parking lot of a bar. When they entered the establishment, a wailing soprano voice threatened to wash them back outside. Karaoke night was in full swing.

"How about a game of darts?" Porter asked.

"I've never played before."

"I'll show you how to hit the bull's-eye." He laid a five-dollar bill on the bar and the bartender handed them two sets of darts. Then Porter stood behind Wendy, grasped her wrist and raised her arm.

"What are you doing?" she whispered, when his breath feathered across the back of her neck.

"Showing you how to throw." He pulled her arm back and then thrust it forward. She released the dart and it sailed across the room, hitting the wall next to the board.

"You're not a very good teacher," she said.

"I'm better at other things." The heat in his eyes stole her breath.

If you kiss him, you'll compromise your investigation.

Right now, she didn't care about her job. All she wanted was to feel Porter's mouth on hers.

He stepped back suddenly. "It's late. We'd better go."

Wendy followed, relieved one of them had come to their senses before it had been too late—she just wished it had been her and not Porter.

Look for A COWBOY OF HER OWN
by Marin Thomas, available January 2015
wherever Harlequin® American Romance®
books and ebooks are sold.

HAREXP0115

HARLEQUIN®

American Romance®

For their son

Texas veterinarian Delaney Blair will do *anything* to find a
bone marrow donor for her four-year-old son, Nickolas.
The only likely match is his Argentinean father, Dario.
But Dario doesn't even know he has a son!

Delaney travels to Argentina to find him, and Dario,
shocked, returns to Texas. It's not long before Nick and
Dario become close. Dario can't hide the feelings he has
for Delaney. Dario's family doesn't want him to be with
her. But now they have to see if the love between them is
strong enough to keep them together.

Look for
TEXAS MOM

by ROZ DENNY FOX,

available January 2015 wherever
Harlequin® American Romance®
books and ebooks are sold.

HAR75552